O
F
A
C
E
S

TWO FACES

FACES

Walking in Two Worlds

George McMullen
Foreword by Abraham Truss

HAMPTON ROADS
PUBLISHING COMPANY, INC.

for the evolving human spirit

Cover design by Marjoram Productions
Illustrations by Abraham Truss

For information write:

Hampton Roads Publishing Company, Inc.
134 Burgess Lane
Charlottesville, VA 22902

Or call: (804)296-2772
FAX: (804)296-5096
e-mail: hrpc@mail.hrpub.com
Web site: http://www.hrpub.com

If you are unable to order this book from your local
bookseller, you may order directly from the publisher.
Quantity discounts for organizations are available.
Call 1-800-766-8009, toll-free.

ISBN 1-57174-071-6

10 9 8 7 6 5 4 3 2 1

Printed on acid-free paper in Canada

To my wife Charlotte
and
my children
Elizabeth, Dennis, and Cindy.

With very special thanks
to
Ann Emerson.

Foreword

George McMullen perceives information by faculties other than normal perception and reflection—by means of paranormal or psychic cognition. By a process which includes inhibiting normal sense stimuli and an effort of will, George can withdraw his mind into an altered state of awareness as a cognitive gateway to nonphysical dimensions that transcend the four-dimensional spatio-temporal system of reference of our ordinary physical environment. The metaphysical concepts of a continuum of discrete states of consciousness and of nonmanifest levels of activity and sources of information and energy beyond human knowledge postulate the existence of innumerable separate dimensional realities other than the external reality of our space-time universe with which we are familiar—multidimensional realities that are entered into and experienced as a function of altering consciousness. A discrete altered state of consciousness can be defined as a dimensional frame of reference. Shifting the state of consciousness shifts the dimensional frame of reference.

An introduction of George McMullen's remarkable talent of psychometry and his accomplishments in the field of psychic archaeology cannot be adequately presented here; the reader is referred to George's book *One White Crow*, which documents George's association with Dr. J. Norman Emerson, Ph.D., who, before his death in November 1978, was Senior Professor of Anthropology and Director of Archaeological Studies at the University of Toronto, where he taught for more than thirty years. Dr. Emerson was the co-founding Vice-President and later President of the Canadian Archaeological Association and was widely regarded as "the father of Canadian archaeology." He was the pioneer in North America in what he called Intuitive Archaeology—an innovative approach of using the abilities of individuals singularly gifted with intuitive powers to describe events caught and frozen in time to get a glimpse of what Emerson called "psychic historical truth," in order, as he expressed it, to put flesh on the bones and to give life and human meaning to the artifacts that archaeologists dig up of past civilizations. Traditional research into human prehistory has a major weakness: there is an inevitable lack of humanity. Real men and women hardly ever tread across the pages of our site reports, conference papers, and written books. As the realms of art, symbolism, social meanings, and individual and societal values are encountered, our ability and confidence vanish. Yet these are all part of the questions which make such a difference when one tries to understand a living person and his culture.

It is precisely this understanding that is the touchstone of George McMullen's books. *Two Faces* is the final book of a trilogy, begun with *Red Snake* and continued with *Running Bear*, which chronicles several generations of a Native American family of the Huron and Mohawk tribes in southern Ontario. Two Faces was the son of Running Bear and the great-grandson of Red Snake. Notwithstanding his successful establishment in the White Man's mercantile community, Two Faces' assimilation was never complete, for he cherished the legacy of traditions and customs of his native heritage, even as the Indian's way of life was disappearing and its cultural roots were withering. Throughout his narrative, written with an engaging blend of candor and sensitivity, Two Faces' perceptiveness, acumen, wit, and wry sense of humor are manifest. The description of his encounter with Born Many Times, Shaman of the Mohawk, is imbued with mystical significance. The Shaman's unusual name alludes to the prophetic implications of his revelational knowledge.

George's books provide a unique insight into the Huron-Iroquois culture which flourished before the arrival of the French explorers. The lives of Red Snake, Running Bear, and Two Faces, portrayed in their psychic communications and George's experiential interaction with their historical reality, resonate with an undeniable validity. Expressing the profound pathos and poignancy of an indigenous people fated for extinction, George has this to say: "I have come to know these people from the past and I can assure you that they felt pain, loved and cared for each other, had dignity, compassion, and intelligence. They had no illegitimate children to put away in orphanages. They had no prisons or poorhouses. They took care of their elderly with respect and love. They believed in and prayed to a Supreme Being and were careful to obey His/Her laws. Perhaps, if we can see and understand who and what they really were in the days gone past, our perception of them would change, and we could benefit from some of their wisdom."

Abraham Truss
Toronto, Ontario

Introduction

This is the story of a man of mixed blood. He was born at the time when the White Man was arriving in large numbers to colonize the New World. At the time of his birth other children too were being born of mixed race; his story is in some sense their story, although not many were able to cope as well as Two Faces.

Knowing he fit in neither society, Two Faces was determined to make his way in both worlds. His philosophy was simple: the White Man was bad and the Indian was good. He believed education was the key to his survival in the White world. He realized that few, if any, settlers who came to the New World were educated, and he was determined to take advantage of this fact.

Naturally the Indians were not educated as far as the White Man's standards were concerned, but they were very well educated in survival and in their own customs. They survived very well for ages before the White Man "discovered" this continent. No one has lived with nature and not been influenced by her whims and fancies; the secret of the Indian's existence was his ability to coexist with nature, and not try to conquer it. Success begets respect, and in this facet of life Two Faces was successful. He did not, however, succeed in gaining the respect of most of the White people with whom he dealt. A few close business acquaintances respected him highly, but only because of his ability to do something for them. Two Faces was wise enough to realize this truth.

His Indian culture allowed him to accomplish things that his White culture could not and vice versa. This made him as "two men" in one body—one face for Indian, one face for White man. Hence his name the Indians gave him. He was fortunate to find a woman who shared his problem, as she too was of two races—Indian and White. Being of mixed blood made it easier for him to accomplish all he did. If he had been of one race, he would have been loyal only to that race.

Two Faces understood both cultures, but his loyalty was stronger to the Indian than to the White. He was not fully accepted by the Indians, however, although many of the most knowledgeable of their leaders sympathized with his situation. With the exception of the Durham family, no White person was truly sympathetic, or tried to understand his predicament.

Unfortunately, the same prejudice exists today. The Metis of Canada are a tribe of mixed Indian and White blood. They are still trying to get recognition from the government on land claims. It is my opinion that one of the most famous Canadian heroes was a Metis by the name of Louis Riel. He was hanged by the British for fighting to protect his people and their land. It is my hope that the story of Two Faces will open a window into the difficult lives endured by the people of mixed race who find themselves in this position through no fault of their own.

Chapter I
Two Faces, Who I Am

My earliest name was Cold Eyes. When I was born my parents, Running Bear and Yellow Flower, gave this name to me. They thought that my eyes gave the appearance of being cold, because they were ice blue in colour. I am a half-breed, or of mixed blood. When my mother was a young girl she was raped by a French trader. She and several other girls had been kidnapped from their camp. Running Bear was with a group of Indians that tracked down the kidnappers and rescued the girls. My mother was an Onondaga and she thought that she could not return to her tribe, because it was a very religious one and she felt she had disgraced them, even though it was no fault of her own.

Later Running Bear took her as his woman and became my father. They had another son that was a full blood. They called him Slow Bear, because he seemed to be very slow in all that he did. Never was any difference shown to me by my parents because I was not a full-blooded Indian. My brother and I were very close and he refused to accept the ceremonies that would mean bringing him into manhood and being named, because their tribe had refused to accept me.

My father worked for an English trader whose name was Mr. Durham. It was in a Trading Post by the lake called Erie, so named by the nearby tribe, although it was actually in Seneca territory. These people were part of a larger group called the Iroquois. My father was a Mohawk, although his grandfather, Red Snake, was a Huron. The Huron had long ago ceased to exist as a tribal force. Their main village of Cahiague had been destroyed by the New York Iroquois, and the people who survived went to other tribes and were assimilated by them. My father went as a captive to the Mohawk and was initiated into that tribe.

Running Bear had traveled far and wide after his grandfather, Red Snake, died and eventually settled down with the trader. He worked hard and was appreciated by him. Unfortunately he contacted a lung disease and died in his forties. We buried him in the forest, not far from the Post. Both my brother and I continued to work for the White trader. Slow Bear hunted and supplied the Post with game, while I worked in the Post and also visited the villages around us, encouraging the Indians to trade at our Post.

The White people began calling me James, an English name, and I made no objection. The White man's woman, Mrs. Durham, started teaching me to read and write in English. I found it easy and proved to be a fast learner. Their son Peter was a few years older than I. He was thin and sickly. He spent most of his time reading and writing. I became friends with him and he taught me many things about English culture that his mother did not teach me. I, in turn, taught him what I knew of Indian ways.

When I was about twelve an older Indian came to the Post and inquired about my mother. I took him to our lodge, which was close by, and called to my mother. When she saw the man, she looked both surprised and concerned. He went to her and took her in his arms and she started to cry. I was about to seize hold of the man, when he stepped back and I saw tears in his eyes too.

"At last I have found you," he said. "Why did you not return to us? Your family thought you were dead and we have grieved for you these many years."

"I felt I had disgraced our family," she answered, and proceeded to explain what had happened to her.

I stood and watched them both as she talked and realized that this man was her father. I also realized that I was the result of her problem, so I turned and started back to the Post, leaving them alone. As I walked away, I felt that indeed I was different from the rest of the Indians and knew they would never accept me. Later, my brother came to the Post and said that my mother wanted me to come to her lodge.

I went with him and when we arrived the man came up to me and hugged me close. I just stood in amazement as he said, "I am happy to meet my other grandson. Your mother has told me what fine sons she has and I can see why."

I said to him, "I am pleased to meet my mother's father," and I could say no more.

It was an embarrassing silence that followed, and it was finally broken by my mother, telling us that we should eat a meal that she had prepared. I looked at Slow Bear, but he kept his head down and I could see that he was deep in thought. I wondered what was in store for us now, because of this strange development. After I had eaten lightly, I made the excuse that I was needed at the Post and left.

I slept in the forest that night, not wanting to disturb my mother and her father. I went to her lodge in the morning and found them in great spirits. They had decided that we were all to go to her village and be with the rest of her family. I told them that I could not go, that I had to stay and work at the Post. They argued with me for some time. Finally I told them that although I preferred the Indian way because of its traditions and customs, I also had White Man's blood and that I must learn their ways too.

This was of course quite a shock to my mother, who at the time could not understand why I wanted this. But her father and Slow Bear understood perfectly well and sided with me against her objections.

I knew that she had a terrible decision to make. I tried to make it as easy as possible for her, by saying I would visit her often. I was now twelve years of age. It was time for me to be on my own and to make my own way.

They took three days in preparing to leave. When the day finally arrived, my mother held me close for some time and then her father held me also. Slow Bear was standing some distance away. When my mother and grandfather came up to him he turned and ran to me, hugging me so tightly that I couldn't breathe. We were both crying, but at the same time trying to show we were both men. We just stood and said nothing, holding each other. Then he turned and quickly left.

When they had gone from sight, I felt ever so alone. I sat in front of the lodge for a long time. Finally, a noise behind me made me turn. There was a young couple with two children, standing behind me. The man approached and asked if I was going to use the lodge to live in. Realizing that they wanted it, I told them to go ahead and move in. They both thanked me and I left, taking what was left there that was mine.

I was amazed that news had spread so fast among the Native people. How did they know my mother was leaving the lodge? It did not matter to me, however, as I had no intention of living there with all the memories it recalled. I was determined to make my own way without any commitments to family or the past. I had been turned down for initiation by our people, so I needed to find my own way among the White people even though they were not really accepting of me either, and even though I preferred Indian ways.

Chapter 2
A New Lifestyle

I returned to the Post and the Durhams knew that I had said goodbye to my family. They were good people. The father had been a merchant in England and the mother had been a schoolteacher. Peter was their only child. When Mr. Durham had a chance to come to the New World, as he called it, they accepted the challenge for a new life. They had known things would be different, but did not expect the hardships they now had.

Of course I could not see how they had any hardships. I thought they had everything that one could wish for—a nice store, a good place to live, and plenty to eat. That was more than most Indians had. They assured me that I could live with them and work, as I had been doing. They looked upon me as another son. I appreciated what they said and I was determined to learn their ways and take what benefit I could from it. I thought that I would never be able to make it in the Indian world, so I would make it in the White Man's.

I quickly adapted to the work again, but with more vigour. I spent every extra minute learning the lessons from Mrs. Durham. I could speak English fairly well and went on to read and write it. But I did not give up my Iroquois tongue. In fact, I took every opportunity to learn other dialects of this language. Mrs. Durham was very proud of my accomplishing the speaking of the different languages and took every chance she could to add to my learning.

In the meantime the store prospered, even though there were other Trading Posts opening nearby. I went from village to village, encouraging the people to trade with us. I threw myself into the commercial side of the business, learning as much as I could.

The Durhams' son Peter helped me in many ways and I would take him with me when we visited the Indian villages around the Post. He soon learned a little of their language and could talk with them. As was usual for an Indian, I had learned quite young about sexual matters and when visiting the villages would take the opportunity to put this knowledge to use. Peter sensed what I was up to and spoke to me about it.

Apparently he had never been with a woman and asked me many questions. It turned out that the best I could do was to arrange for him to have a woman in trade. In other words, he would give the woman some kind of gift. This could be a comb, a reflecting glass, or something from the Trading Post. He quickly produced something from the Post, so I arranged for a woman who had lost her man to satisfy him.

They met one evening in the bush near the Trading Post and he was gone for some time. Later the woman told me that he was very shy and still a virgin, so she had to take her time with him. It appeared that he was quite taken with this activity, so he was always giving me items from the store for me to trade for the girls' favors. I then took advantage of this situation, by upping the price for a girl's use. I soon accumulated a good supply of combs, mirrors, coloured cloth, and beads.

It seemed as if Peter was never satisfied. He was in the bush every night. If they had been White girls, he might not have been so active. In any event, his father soon became suspicious about his activity in the bushes and watched him closely. Finally one night his mother and father called us into the store and told us that they were sending Peter to England to finish his education. They then surprised me by saying that they wished me to accompany him in order to take care of him.

This meant that I would see the land of the White Man and receive further education as well. Here was an opportunity that I had no intention of refusing. Not many Indian boys—let alone a half-breed—were given a chance like this. I accepted at once and plans were made for the trip.

Chapter 3
The Land of the White Man

After much planning, the arrangements were completed. Mrs. Durham made new clothes for me, so I looked very much like a White person. I found the clothes confining, but was determined to wear them regardless. The pants and stockings were new to me and the white shirt with its lace trim made me feel feminine. The shoes seemed to be too big and heavy, but were something that I knew I had to get used to.

On a spring morning we left for a coastal town, where we boarded a company boat that was getting ready to sail for England. We were to travel with a shipment of furs and other items from the Trading Post. The boat was bigger than I had expected, and had large white sails. There were more White people on board ship than I had ever seen before in one place. The activity was bedlam, with orders flying and people running in all directions, or so it seemed to me. This was only a small taste of what was to come.

Peter and I were given a tiny cabin amidship, which was not large enough for even one person. I was to learn later that this was one of the bigger cabins, given to us because of the Captain's friendship with Mr. Durham. It took another day to finish loading the ship; then the following morning we sailed away from port. Soon things quieted down and the only sound was an occasional song from some seaman or an order being given.

The meals were strange to me, being mostly a very thin soup with a hard roll. Once a day we all lined up for a small tin cup filled with what the sailors called a ration of rum. This was a very harsh drink and difficult for me to swallow. Peter said that I was to think of it as medicine to avoid seasickness. In my mind it would cause it, rather than prevent it. I was told that this drink could become habit-forming and could ruin your life, if it became necessary to have it. Later in my life I was to learn that some Indians would kill, just to get some of it.

I spent most of my time talking with the sailors. They told me that they had traveled all over the oceans and about what all they had seen. I thought they were just telling tales, but they seemed sincere. One man told me about a country that was situated below my own country, where a tribe of Indians had great wealth at one time. People from a country not far from their own had taken most of this wealth and killed many Indians. He told me that my people were lucky they had the English instead of the Spanish to deal with and had only furs instead of gold.

I could not understand how a metal called gold could be more valuable than furs. It seemed to me that furs were important to the White Man, or else why did the English and the French fight for them so much? I knew little about metal other than the ones I had seen, which were iron, copper, and brass. I had once seen a necklace on a Frenchman the colour of copper and was told that it was gold.

On the second day at sea I found Peter hanging over the rail, bringing up what he had eaten and trying to bring up what he had not. He was a peculiar colour and the brunt of jokes from the sailors. Luckily I did not catch whatever it was that he had. To me, the weather was perfect. In the afternoons I would lie on a hatch cover in the sun, thinking of how much my life was changing. I was enthusiastic about going to school in the White Man's world and the chance to learn their ways. I was sure it would bring me advantages.

I felt confused in my mind as to whether I was Indian or White. I was not accepted by either, but I still had to belong somewhere. I was told by Indians that came to the Post that many half-breeds were being born in all the tribes and though they had been accepted, they could not join in any of the ceremonies. Deep down, I wanted to be accepted by one or the other of them, but suspected I would not be. Therefore, I determined I would make my own way in both of their societies and felt sure education was the key.

The trip to England took a little over two weeks, with some days when the weather was bad and there was little breeze to fill the sails. The Captain was a good sailor and was very interested in Peter and to me. He listened with interest to our stories of the Trading Post. His stories were all of the sea. When he was a young man living in a coastal city, his family knew that he would go to sea, just as members of his family had always done. He worked hard to become the master of his own ship and had known many hard times.

When we had docked at a place called Liverpool, we were told to stay on board ship for our own protection, because there were many bad characters around the dock. We waited until a carriage with two men arrived. They took us to a lodging house for the night, since it was a day's trip to the school. The city was dark and dirty. A terrible smell filled the air wherever we went. It was the smell of the open sewers that ran along the curbs everywhere. Together with the garbage and excrement of humans and animals, it was very unpleasant to two boys from a clean outside environment.

The next morning we awoke early and were given a hot drink and a sweet bun, with a piece of cheese. I could not eat the cheese, but Peter ate it with great relish. Two men in a carriage with two horses were ready to take us away when we were finished eating.

We wound along narrow laneways between buildings that were made of square red stones. People leaned from the window openings, calling to others on the street.

Many threw water out, to land on anyone passing below. It was altogether an unnerving experience for me.

When we came to the countryside, there was a nice change. The air was clean and fresh. Many trees had flowers on them and I was told they were the blossoms of fruit trees.

There were small homes and buildings where they kept animals. In fields there were horses, cattle, and sheep. There were pigs in small pens, along with chickens and geese, which I had never seen before. My education was beginning even before I reached the school.

We stopped at midday at a place called an inn. Here we were given a meal which consisted of a stew with meat and many kinds of vegetables, along with as much bread as we could eat. It was served with large containers of a drink called ale. We ate from wooden boards with a knife and spoon, which were made of pewter. The drinking containers were also made of pewter. I soon managed to use the utensils, but found it different from using my hands to put food in my mouth as had been my way until then.

We were soon on the road again with another pair of fresh horses. They had changed the animals while we ate. The two men rode up on the front of the carriage, while we had the inside to ourselves. Peter fell asleep, but I could not, with so much to see and learn about. I watched the country go by with interest. I saw a man with two horses making a rough ditch in the ground with a wooden thing with a metal tip. I was later to learn that he was ploughing the ground before planting. I also learned that he did not own the land, but worked for an important man who lived in an immense house on the property.

Toward dusk we turned into a lane between tall trees that led to a large building. We were informed that this was the school and it was where we would live for the next three years.

When we had alighted from the carriage, they took us and our luggage into the building. Inside was a large room with many doors leading out of it. A man came through the doorway near the end of the room and waved for us to follow him. We were taken into an office where a very stern-looking man sat behind a desk.

He informed us that he was the headmaster and that his name was Mr. Graves. He asked us our names and we answered Peter and James Durham. He looked at me carefully, then asked if I was the one that was part Indian.

I told him I was. He then told me I would have no problem, unless I caused them with my heathen ways. I could not understand what heathen ways meant, and did not ask, but kept quiet. He pulled a cord that was hanging behind his desk and another man came into the room. Mr. Graves told him to show us to our rooms.

We left this building and walked along paths, passing several other buildings until we came to one beside a high stone wall. Here we stopped and were taken inside and shown to our rooms. Peter and I had separate rooms, side by side, with a connecting door to allow us into each other's room. There was a bed with coverings and a pillow, a small table, and one chair. A shelf ran along one wall, where we were to put our belongings, with a rod which allowed us to hang our clothes. Under the bed was a chamber pot, that we had to take outside to dump. There was one washroom on each floor. This washroom had a big sink for washing ourselves and our clothing. We had to get the water from a large tank outside that had a pail provided.

The chamber pot was to be dumped into a tank outside. It was taken away every day by a man with a team of horses who picked them up all around the school. We were told there was a stream nearby that we could walk to if we wanted to bathe. I was glad to hear this, as Indians made a habit of bathing each day, while sometimes the White people never seemed to wash at all.

We were allowed to walk through the grounds around the school and even go outside the grounds with special permission. I never had any trouble leaving, as I would go over the wall any time I wanted. The school had a large library of books, where I was to spend the greater part of my spare time during the next three years. Peter also loved to read and did the same. The clothes we wore on arrival were taken from us and stored, to be returned to us when we left the school. We had to wear a sort of school uniform while we were there. I did not mind this because it made it easier for me to blend in with the rest of the boys.

The classes started the next morning and the teachers made us aware that this was not fun and games. We had a long day's schedule, six days a week. Both Peter and I were enrolled in the business and commercial classes, which was our own choice, but also was what was expected by the Trading Company. I found the classes to be easier than I had anticipated because of my experience at the Trading Post and Mrs. Durham's teachings.

The first day we were assessed by the Entrance Committee to decide where we should begin our studies and, thanks again to Mrs. Durham, we were placed into the advanced classes.

I could speak English and French quite fluently and also write these languages with no problem, so this helped me no end. I could also speak and write Iroquois, but this did not help me there, although the teaching staff found it to be amusing.

There were not only classes; we were soon put into sports as well. I was put into a game called rugby, which was a rough-and-tumble game. It appeared the best players were the ones that inflicted the most injuries on the opposition. I was continually bruised and scratched while playing. I soon learned a painful lesson when I was kicked in the crotch by an opposing player.

It appeared that if you could not kick the football, you were expected to kick the other two balls between the opposing player's legs. After I was kicked, I lay in pain for some time, wondering if I would ever be the same again. Another player helped me to my feet. He later told me that an ironmonger in town made a tin cup that his wife would then line with cotton. This device was worn over your crotch to protect yourself.

The next time I was in town, I bought one of these and wore it when playing. Even then, after every game, I had to bang the dents out before wearing it again. I soon learned to do my share of kicking, biting, scratching, elbowing, and butting. They did this for fun and competition. White Man said that the Indians were uncivilized. I could not see that rugby was a civilized game the way they played it. To be fair, we Indians played a game called lacrosse by the French. This game could be very violent too. Peter was put into the more gentlemanly game of cricket. This meant no bodily contact whatever.

Unfortunately for Peter and me, as well as the other boys, there were no females in the school. After a few weeks I had to find a way to correct this. Being raised in an area where Indian villages were, it was an easy matter to keep active sexually. The White people were very primitive in this matter. I talked to some of the senior boys and was told that women were available in the nearby city. I was also told these women expected hard money for this service. Peter and I were on a limited budget, so it meant that only one of us could make a trip to the city for this purpose, and only once a month. After living as we had near the Indian villages, where we could get this service for a few trinkets that we took from the Trading Post, it was quite a hardship.

Chapter 4
I Start a Business

Somehow I had to find a way to get the service that Peter and I were used to having for less money. The first time I went to the city, I found the available women in a certain area, which was in a rather rundown district. The woman I chose was not old, as most of them were. She took me to a very shabby room where we did the business. Afterwards I asked her if she made much money. She said hardly enough to make it worthwhile. The most business came from the school. Suddenly I had an idea. I asked her, if she were to be guaranteed a fixed number of clients a night, would she be willing to charge less? I told her that she would be making much more money than she was now. She was interested.

I told her that I could build her a small lodge behind the rear wall of the school and would supply all the clients necessary to keep her busy all night. She said she had nothing to lose and all to gain, but wanted to bring another girl with her for security. I agreed to this and told her that I would be in touch.

At the next chance I got, I searched and found a very secluded spot in the bushes near the wall. Here I built a very good lodge, about ten by fifteen feet in size. It was built the way of the Indian in the New World, except I scrounged the lumber from an old building that stood near the stream. I was told that this was an abandoned mill. The walls of the lodge were made of poles, set side by side, into the ground. There was no shortage of these in the forest nearby. I laid the borrowed lumber from the mill across the poles for the roof. On top of this, I put a thick matting of grass sod, which made the roof leakproof. I used a door made from lumber that I took from the mill and also a window, which I repaired. Peter and another boy helped me build the lodge. It took us three weeks to finish it. We made the beds from lumber and the mattresses of linen, filled with straw. Later, I had a rough stone fireplace made for cooking. Light was supplied by candles, which were common in those days. I managed to scrounge enough bed coverings from the school to supply the beds. We made two, but had them separated by a wall.

I was now ready for business. I told all the boys what I had done and then lined up clients for the girls. The boys were so happy to be able to climb the wall, get what they wanted, then climb back over the wall again without having the trip to the city that they said they were willing to pay extra for this service. I then went to town and contacted the girls, who agreed to meet me at a specified place.

That night I climbed the wall and met them as we had agreed. I took them to the lodge and they were delighted. I told them what the price would be and that I would collect the money from the clients, and pay them later.

This arrangement meant that the boys were paying more for what I was supplying. It also meant a handsome profit for me and naturally I could help myself to the service for free. I know that I would be considered a pimp, but I felt no guilt over this. The girls were better off than before; the boys had a convenience and I had a profit. Anyway, I was in this school to learn business and this is what I was doing. The girls were going to do what they were doing, regardless of me. In a way, it was my revenge on the White people, who had done this very thing to Indian girls ever since they had come to my country.

Business was very brisk. It passed my expectations. I had funds to spare and soon had to enlarge the lodge and bring in two more girls. I had to pay off some security police from the school, but it was no problem. Peter was aware of what I was doing and thought it was hilarious. He was one of my best customers.

Business was so good that I began to look for something close by that was larger to use instead of the lodge. I found a vacant house on a farm about a half mile from the school, so I went to see the owner. He lived in another house on the farm and I made my way there. When the man opened the door, I was surprised to find that it was one of the sailors that worked on the boat that we had come to England on. He remembered me and invited me into the house.

The home was sparsely furnished and I was to learn that he was not married. He told me that he had been left the farm by his parents and since he did not like farming, he had gone to work at sea. I told him of my interest in his other house and was honest with him as to why I wanted it. He began to laugh and then laughed so much that he had a choking fit. After he had regained his breath, he told me that the school frowned on this type of thing, as did the community.

He told me that a minister lived beside the church, about two miles down the road from the house. It delighted his sense of humor to think of my proposal. We talked about it for over three hours. When we were finished, we had an agreement. One stipulation was that he be employed by me as a caretaker and general maintenance person. He said this was to protect his property, but I knew he relished the thought of the availability of the girls.

I quickly hired people to make the necessary changes to the house, so by the time it was finished I had room for six girls—two more than I had before. The furnishings were an improvement that my clientele seemed to appreciate. Again the business prospered beyond my expectations. I hired Peter to keep the books and to make sure everyone was paid off. He loved his job and spent every spare moment at the house.

There was a gardener—a bachelor—that lived on the school property in a small secluded cottage, set back in some trees. He became a good customer, as did some of the members of the faculty. There were other men besides the students using the facility. I kept Peter busy changing all my share of the proceeds into gold coins, which were easier to hide away. You could not trust anyone to keep your money secure in this type of business.

Eventually the headmaster, Mr. Graves, heard rumors of my business endeavor and called me before him. He asked me if the rumor was true. I had no choice but to confess. He questioned me closely about everything to do with the business and asked if any of his staff used my facilities. I told him I would never betray such confidences. He then surprised me by asking if there was any way he could use this facility without anyone finding out. I told him I would make the necessary arrangements and only he and I would know.

How I was to accomplish this I had no idea. As I walked to my lodging I passed by the gardener's bungalow. I thought for a minute and then had a brilliant idea. I went to the bungalow and was admitted by the gardener. I asked him if I could use his house for two hours one night a week and offered him any girl in the house for this privilege. He agreed so fast that I was startled. I made the arrangement for every Wednesday night.

I hurried back to the Headmaster's office. Luckily he was still there. I informed him of my plan and he was delighted. He agreed on the time and day. I then confirmed this with the gardener, who asked me who the person was that was to use his bungalow. I told him I was sworn to secrecy. He agreed never to come near the bungalow at the time and day agreed upon.

I picked one of the better girls to make this rendezvous and swore her to secrecy as to who her client was to be. I promised her dire circumstances if she did not keep her tongue still. She laughed and said that she and the other girls were happy that I had made it possible for them to make so much money and that she had no desire to jeopardize anything.

Everything worked beautifully for Mr. Graves and he was a very pleased Headmaster, as far as I was concerned. Neither he nor any of the staff interfered with me or my business, thereafter. The sailor, Mr. Carruthers, was happy with the arrangements. He enjoyed himself immensely, especially when he recognized the minister of the local church, dressed in disguise, using the facility a few times. No one said anything about this and the minister never suspected we knew him.

One day Mr. Carruthers told me there was to be an auction of livestock at a nearby farm and asked me if I was interested in buying a riding horse. He said that there was an excellent horse to be sold off. Not knowing anything about horses, I went along with him to the auction. It was to be held on the following Saturday morning at a nearby estate. We walked there in about two hours. It was a beautiful day and many people were present. As the owner of the stock was a high-born person, it meant that the stock would be the best.

We watched as cattle, sheep, and goats were sold. Then came the horses. I would have bid on any one of them, but Carruthers stayed my hand. Near the end of the auction, a black horse was brought in and Carruthers said this was the one. The bidding started low, but built up quickly. Another man and I were finally the only two bidding. He was also one of the gentry and was bound to have his way. Every time he bid, I bid higher and finally he became very angry and demanded to know who I was and if I possessed that kind of money.

Carruthers informed him that I was a very rich person from the Colonies and that I was buying the stallion for breeding purposes. He still demanded proof that I had the money to pay, because it was to be cash purchases only. I pulled a bag of gold coins from my pocket and dumped some into my hand. Most of the people gasped when they saw the coins and realized by the size of the bag that there was a large amount. I then asked him to produce proof that he had enough money to pay what he was bidding. Since he had obviously bought a considerable quantity of animals, he said he did not have the money on him, but that many people there knew he was a man of circumstance. The auctioneer said that since the man could not produce what he had asked me to, the animal therefore was sold to Mr. James Durham.

The man was very angry, but later came over to me and apologized. He said he had wanted the horse ever since it had been born and was disappointed he was not getting it.

I told him that the horse was not that important to me and if he wished to make me a suitable deal, then he could have the horse. He looked incredulous and quickly made me an offer of two horses that he had. I asked if that included harness, bridles, and saddles, and he agreed. We made arrangements to go to his farm the next day.

When Carruthers and I reached his farm the following day, the man was more than happy to see us. He said that he had feared that I would change my mind overnight. He did not seem to realize, nor do other White men, that an Indian never took his word lightly, even a half-breed Indian.

With much pride, he showed us the house and stable. He had many fine animals besides horses. His favorite hobby was the breeding of cattle and he had won many prizes for his stock. He had the two horses brought out for me to examine. Carruthers looked at them for me, since I was not that familiar with these creatures. He said that both appeared to be sound and asked to ride them before making up his mind. The owner agreed and had his stable help saddle one for him. Carruthers was gone for over an hour. When he returned, he was well pleased with the animal. He then took the other horse for a ride and took just as long with this one. In the meantime his Lordship had me come to the house, where we were served a hot drink and some flat pastries called cookies. He spent this time telling me about his ancestors and how they were so important in battles for the Monarchy. He lost me there and I just politely nodded as he talked.

I was relieved when Carruthers returned, giving us the excuse to leave with the two horses. I was not used to riding and Carruthers told me what to do. We went to where the girls were and stabled the horses in a small barn behind the house. Carruthers said that he would take personal care of the animals, which gave me relief. Both Peter and I spent many days riding and soon decided which one we favored. They were both rather large beasts, but accustomed to man. The one I rode was young and a little headstrong, but once he got used to me he was gentle.

I had made many improvements in the house to make it more attractive for the girls to work in. Carruthers was continually busy repairing and building. I had new chairs and sofas added to the reception room where the clients could be served a drink and light food, such as cakes and sandwiches. They paid for these, of course, and I profited.

One day Carruthers told me that a woman wanted to talk with me. I went over to the house and met a lady whom I guessed to be in her thirties. She was not unattractive, but was extremely thin. She wanted to work in the house with the younger girls. I asked her why and she told me she had been abandoned by her husband and had no place to live, or any other way to make a living.

I talked this over with Carruthers, who was, I could see, taken with the lady. It was decided that we would give her a position, but not servicing clients, as the younger girls did. She could help make the meals and do the laundry for the house, though not the clothes of the girls.

Two Faces

There was much work needing to be done about the place, including cleaning the candle lamps daily and washing the pots and pans.

She was also to discipline the girls and make them get along together, sort of as a den mother. We made the offer to her and she was pleased to accept. I don't think she really wanted to be used by men.

I heard complaints from the police officers, whom we had to pay off, that many of the ladies of the night in the nearby city were not happy with us for taking so much of their business away. I had expanded my house to where I now had more than twelve girls. Peter was so busy with the bookkeeping that his studies were getting neglected. I was able to keep up with my school work with no problem because I had more incentive to do so.

In no time at all, it seemed, the three years of school were over. I had made a considerable amount of money and did not want to see it end. They held a big ceremony where they gave those of us who had succeeded in passing a very important-looking document. Mr. Graves said a few words to every recipient. When I received mine, he said there was no doubt that I would succeed in the business world, wherever I located. However, he did not know the Colonies as I did.

Peter and I made arrangements to return to the New World, as they called it. The clothes made by Mrs. Durham that we had worn when we arrived were much too small for us, for we had filled out since our arrival. We went to a tailor and had clothes custom made to fit us. We were not without funds to do this in the proper way, befitting our position as young gentlemen of means.

I sold the business to Carruthers, who by now had married the lady who had come to us looking for a position. He paid me a small sum down and promised to send payments to the New World, as often as he could manage. He kept his word, until some ten years later when he was killed by a rival owner of a house in town.

Chapter 5
Homeward Bound

I made arrangements for my horses to be loaded onto the boat that we were to sail home on. It cost me a goodly sum, but the animals now meant a lot to me. On a day with a sky that was heavy with clouds and with falling rain, we said our goodbyes to everyone. It was surprising the number of friends we had made during the three years we had spent there. Many of our fellow students were showing an interest in coming to the New World to live.

Once on board ship, I made sure the animals were taken care of. The boat was loaded with trade goods and furniture. There were several large trunks that belonged to us and to the other passengers taken aboard. The Captain requested my presence in his cabin. He told me that because I was an Indian, my trip would be made below decks and also that I would not be able to mingle with the White passengers. He said an important official of the Trading Company was on board and it would be better if we made no contact.

Peter was outraged over this and I was angry too. The area that was given to me was where the least important members of the crew were billeted. *Very well, Mr. Captain*, I thought. *I will accept this insult.* I made up my mind that he would somehow pay for this. The first thing that I did, with the help of Peter, was to find the ship's manifest, showing what items were being carried to the New World.

I spent three days checking cargo against the manifest and knew then that the captain was skimming from the top. In other words, he was carrying things that were not shown on the manifest; therefore he was taking this material to the New World to sell privately. I made a request for the Captain to grant me an audience. After four days at sea and with Peter's help, the audience was granted.

I was taken to his cabin by a mate and after we were alone, I told the Captain what I had found. I thought the man was going to try to kill me on the spot. He calmed down when I told him that Peter was sitting by the Company official, waiting to see what happened to me. If anything did, he would report my findings to the official. There would be no difficulty for the Company to prove my findings, once we docked and they examined the cargo.

With an effort, the Captain smiled and said, "Now young man, we all have to make a little extra when we can, so perhaps we can come to a mutual agreement."

I replied, "I am always open to some arrangement."

He said, "Perhaps you could tell me what you have in mind?"

"I believe, first of all, that you should put me into a cabin on the upper deck," I said, "and further than that, I want to estimate the value of your contraband. I expect that I should get twenty-five percent of this value, paid in gold, by the time we dock."

Again, he almost exploded and said there could be no deal. I got up to leave. He asked if I would take a little less. I told him I would take no less than twenty percent of my value estimate. This time he agreed. He called the mate to take me to the upper deck, where I was given a cabin next to Peter. When Peter saw me he laughed with pleasure, for he knew I had won.

The mate had my belongings brought up to my cabin. The next day Peter and I were busy estimating the value of the material that was not on the manifest. It was not all that great, but still I would make quite a tidy sum.

Chapter 6
The Company Official

That night at the evening meal, with the Captain present, I was introduced to the official of the Trading Company. He was going to the New World as an observer and then was to report back to the head office in London.

He was accompanied by his wife, a very charming woman. He asked me where I had been on the boat up until now and I replied that I was taking care of my animals and helping the Captain with his manifest. He inquired about my horses and I learned that he was very interested in them. The Captain excused himself and left the table. The official's wife asked to be excused also.

The three of us talked over a glass of ale for a few hours, mostly about Trading Posts and the Indians. He made us aware that he knew of our scholastic records, as he had contacted the school before leaving England. Peter left the table after making an excuse about being a little seasick.

The official, whose name was Mr. Butler, questioned me further about the Trading Post and particularly about my past. I was beginning to be uncomfortable and, noticing this, he put his cards on the table.

"I know everything about you, James," he said. "I know that you are of a mixed race and all your family details. Mr. Carruthers once worked for me and he supplied me with interesting details of your business adventure while in school. I am not here to criticize you, or what you did. I want to offer you a position as my assistant in the New World." I was surprised by his frankness and knew he was one smart person. Could I work for such a man? I wondered.

Almost reading my mind, he said, "This is not just an ordinary position, but one that takes a person with your talents. The Company suspects that our traders are not always honest in their work and are skimming profits from the Company. Your job would be to uncover these practises and report them to me."

I wanted to question his statement about a man with my talents, but let it pass. Instead, I told him that I would require time to think about his offer. He told me I had about two weeks to think about it before we docked in the New World. He also suggested that there were many benefits for me besides money in this position. I took this to mean that I would be given my own Post to run.

It was necessary for me to clean the stalls of the horses and throw the manure overboard every day. I did this around the same time each morning. About a week after my discussion with the Captain, I went to the hold where the horses were kept. Suddenly I heard a noise behind me and turned to see the mate with a club in his hand, about to swing at my head. I moved as quickly as I could, but still took a glancing blow to my shoulder. Ducking low, I plunged into him and we both fell to the floor, with me on top of him.

He grabbed at my face and eyes and I hit him in the groin with a short jab. He grunted and fell back again, and this time I hit him in the neck, just below his chin. His face turned red and he started to choke. I pulled him to his feet and hit him again in the nose. He fell backward between the horses. I grabbed him and shoved his face into the manure and then stepped back.

He lay there coughing, holding his broken nose, with his face covered in horse dung. I pulled him to the side, then cleaned the horses stall, as though he were not even there. I fed and watered the horses and then threw water on the mate, who was now groaning in pain. I told him I could very easily kill him and I would, if he came near me or my horses again.

I went up on deck and looked for the Captain, who was in his cabin as usual. I entered without knocking and he jumped to his feet at my appearance. I had scratches on my face and manure on my clothes, so he knew I had been in a fight. I told him that the mate was in trouble down on the deck by the horses and required attention. I also said that he got off lucky this time, but I would kill him if he came near me again. I then told him that the information I had regarding his manifest was in a letter in the possession of Mr. Butler and would be read if anything happened to me.

I went straight to Peter's cabin and told him what had happened. He laughed and said he felt that something like this could happen. He had not worried about me, for he had seen many times that I could take care of myself. I went to my cabin and cleaned myself up. I lay on the bunk for an hour or so, then went up on deck and lay in the sun. The sky was as blue as I had ever seen it. I thought of all the things that had happened to me in the past three years. My thoughts then turned to my mother and brother and I wondered how they were. I decided then to take the position with Mr. Butler.

I was not bothered for the rest of the trip, but I kept a wary eye out. Peter was with me when I attended the horses. Mr. Butler was pleased that I was taking the position with him and he filled me in on details of what he expected of me.

I was free to travel to the various Trading Posts and would carry a letter of identification that would explain to the Post managers about my duties and also give me the authority to examine any and all documents of the Trading Company.

After a very smooth voyage we finally reached the Trading Company's docks. As I left the ship, the Captain, unseen by anyone else, pressed a small leather bag into my hand.

I saw to the unloading of the horses and their gear before we went to the offices of the Trading Company. Mr. Butler had been given a warm welcome by the other officials and he introduced me and Peter to them. He informed them that I would be working for him and was to answer to him alone. No one was to interfere with me because I would be carrying out his instructions.

I could see that many were surprised, because they could tell I was a half-breed and they did not trust anyone with Indian blood. Peter and I were given lodging in a rooming house that was nearby. We stayed only the night there and next morning we said our goodbyes to the Butlers. We each had a horse to ride and had no problems with our luggage, which would be shipped to the Durham Trading Post. We carried only what we would need on the journey.

Chapter 7
A Family Reunion

After a few days, Peter and I parted company. He took the road to the Trading Post. I wanted to go to the village where my mother and brother were living. After ten days of travel through bush and along animal trails, I arrived in the territory of the Onondaga. I was easily directed to the village of my mother, for many people knew my grandfather. They showed no surprise that I was a half-breed, dressed in White man's clothing and riding a fine horse.

When I entered my mother's village, people came running more to see the horse than me. When my mother saw me she gave a cry and nearly knocked me to the ground as she rushed to embrace me. She seemed to hold me forever, and when she released me I was grabbed by my grandfather in a big bear hug.

Slow Bear was nowhere to be seen and my grandfather told me he was away on a hunt. I was taken into their lodge at once and questions began about where I had been and what had happened to me. I talked for over an hour, explaining all that I had done. The horse was also explained, but when I told them I had two of them, they stared in disbelief.

I told them that Peter had gone on ahead with the other horse to the Trading Post. I explained very briefly about my new position with the Company, not saying anything about questioning the traders' honesty. I showed them the impressive-looking certificate that I had been given at the school and they thought it looked pretty. It was no use trying to explain what it meant; they would not have understood what I was talking about.

When Slow Bear appeared, he also hugged me and kept slapping me affectionately on the back. We dearly loved one another. I gave them all a gold coin from the bag that the Captain had given me. It was of no real value to them, other than for the likeness it had of the English king on it. I could have saved money by just giving them a picture. I told them they could buy things at the Trading Post with it, but they said they would keep it forever. We talked most of the night and finally fell asleep exhausted. It was good that I was exhausted, for it made it easier to sleep on furs again, instead of the beds that I had become accustomed to.

When I awakened I saw that my mother had a meal ready for us and again we talked all morning. I asked Slow Bear if he would like to work for me and the Trading Company. I explained that all he had to do was travel with me to the different Trading Posts.

He would go ahead of me and question the Indians who were leaving the Post after doing business there. He was to find out what they had traded and what they had received. He was to tell the Indians that he had furs to trade and wanted to find the best place to do so. I told him what he would receive for this position and that he would also have a horse to ride as long as he was working for me.

Slow Bear thought I was crazy to pay him for doing so little. He did not realize how important the job was, or the information that he would gather would be for me to have before I arrived at the Posts. He agreed to try out this position for a period, to see if he liked it. My grandfather then asked me if I would join the ceremony with Slow Bear to be named and brought into manhood. I thought he was kidding me, as he knew I was a half-breed, not a full-blooded Indian. He said he had spoken with the Chiefs and the Shaman and they had agreed to allow this.

I asked Slow Bear what he thought about it. He said that he would agree to it, but only if I also agreed. It was therefore decided that we would go through the ceremony the following evening. This meant that my mother, with the help of other women, had to make the garments necessary for me for the ceremony. They worked on the clothes all night and all the next day, getting them finished about two hours before the ceremony was to start.

By the time the ceremony was to begin, most of the tribe were gathered around the sacred firepit. The Shaman called me first, because I was the oldest. He said the name Cold Eyes was what my parents had given me when I was born. The Chief came forward with his ceremonial robes and feathered bonnet and asked me my name, which I gave him. He asked me if my father was named Running Bear and my mother Yellow Flower. I said this was so. He then called my grandfather forward and asked him what was to be my new name. My grandfather said it was to be Two Faces, because I had one face for the Indian and one face for the White Man. Because I had the blood of both within me, I could speak for both people. "But," he said, "you must remember that Running Bear became your father and so you must speak with honesty for the Indian and know there is no honesty in the White Man." There was a murmur in the crowd, as they were wondering what I was going to say to that.

"My brothers," I said, "you are correct to say that there is no honesty in the White people, for you have all suffered from their greed, in the White Man's taking of your land, in the White Man's taking of your women. Rest assured that I take my revenge in my own way upon these people. You look at a man who was created a "no man" in the eyes of either the Indian or the White Man.

"To survive, I have become educated in the White Man's school, and while I have lived among them I have learned their ways. I now become an Indian in manhood and named in this ceremony tonight. I know the Indian ways and they are the ways that I love above all else.

"Many of you do not know," I continued, "that my great-grandfather was Red Snake, a Huron, whose tribe was destroyed by the White Man; and my grandfather, Three Eyes, was also a Huron, who was killed fighting a war brought about by the White Man. Also know that my father was a Huron who had Mohawk blood in him through my great-grandmother, Fawn, the wife of Red Snake. My father, Running Bear, was raised by the Mohawk. The White Man has brought disaster upon me and my ancestors since they arrived in our country. Do not question for one moment where my loyalty lies."

There was a long silence and then there was a loud roar of approval from the people. My grandfather, the Chief, and the Shaman all gave me a hug and many people come forward to squeeze my arm and hands. Never again did I feel so accepted and how much I belonged, as I did that night. Slow Bear was called next and went through the ceremony. It was with honor to my father that he was ceremonially named Slow Bear, the name that Running Bear had given him. After his ceremony he was asked to speak.

He said, "My people, you have heard from my brother, Two Faces, who has told you how proud he is of our heritage and I say to you that I am also proud not only of our heritage, but of my brother. We were raised by loving parents who treated us with no difference, because he had mixed blood and I was full blood, for they loved us both equally. I say as you have accepted him, you have accepted me."

Again, there was a roar from the people and Slow Bear was shown great affection. Mother was very proud of her sons at this moment and Grandfather had tears in his eyes, as he held his daughter close to him. There was feasting and dancing into the late hours of the night and when I finally went to my furs, I slept soundly. The next morning, we made arrangements to leave. Slow Bear packed only a few belongings and I put on Indian clothes, for they made me feel a lot freer. The White Man's clothes were too restrictive and the three-pointed hat kept falling off.

Chapter 8
I Come upon an Orphan

We left the village about midday and went to the northwest. We followed a trail for the first two days, then Slow Bear wanted to proceed by himself. He promised to meet me at the Durhams' Trading Post. With a horse to ride, it was more difficult to follow some of the trails with their steep ravines and high hills. I went more to the north toward a fresh-water lake, passing at the top end of the Cayuga territory.

One evening as I sat by the firepit, cooking a bird that I had killed earlier, I heard a sound in the brush behind me. Not looking in that direction, I went into the bush on the opposite side, then crept around to get behind whatever was there. It was hard to see, because it was so black. Suddenly, I saw a small form behind a tree, observing my fire. I silently approached the figure and when close enough grabbed at it. There was an instant reaction, as the person exploded into a violent fight to free itself from my grasp.

I held on and dragged it to the firelight. What a dirty, bedraggled little creature met my eyes! The face was so smeared with dirt that I could not recognize it as a human. It was framed by long tangled hair and the smell from it was overpowering. I told whatever it was to calm down, as I had no desire to hurt it. After struggling for a few moments, it sat down and became quiet. I looked at it and realized that it was but a child. What kind or type, I could not tell. I offered it some food, which it grabbed from my hand and consumed quickly.

I laughed at the poor little wretch and gave it all the food left and some water to drink. It seemed to gulp it down all at once. It was apparent the poor thing was starving. After a while it appeared to sit very still and I knew that the fire warmth and the food had made the poor creature sleepy. I covered it with some furs and let it be. I kept the fire going all night and watched my guest. On the first light of day, the bundle stirred and became instantly afraid of something. I spoke in a soothing tone and offered more food.

It was taken with some reluctance, or shyness. After eating, the person made as if to leave and I held it back, but it was only going to relieve itself. I watched and when it squatted on the ground, I realized that it was a female. When she came back by the firepit, I pulled her hair from her face. It was a very thin face, with a pair of scared, big eyes that looked back at me. I smiled and stroked her cheek and she seemed to relax some.

I asked her who she was, after finding the dialect of our language that she could understand. She said her father was an Oneida, and that her mother had died at her birth. Her father traded with the White Man for a drink that made him lose his mind and when that happened, he beat her. I was to find out that she was a half-breed like me and her mother had often traded herself for White men's goods. As she had died at childbirth, the father blamed the girl for his woman's death. He continually beat the child and his tribe had eventually exiled him from their territory.

By then the sun was up and the air was warm. I asked her to come to a small stream nearby and she followed me. When I took off my clothes and entered the water, she just stared at me. I asked her to come into the water also. At first she hesitated. Finally, she realized that she had not washed for a long time, which was evident by the smell, so she threw off her furs and joined me. I observed that she was very thin and there were scars on her back and thighs. I tried to guess how old she was. Her breasts were nothing more than small bumps and there was just the beginning of pubic hair, so I thought that she must be about seven years old.

After we had washed, we returned to camp. I gave her some clothes to wear—the shirt and pants that I had made for me in England. The pants hung to her ankles, but at least she was covered and clean. I asked her where her father's camp was and she led me to a small lake, some distance from where we had been. She pointed out a small lean-to. I went there and looked inside while she stayed in the brush. A man was sleeping on some dirty furs. He smelled of rum, the drink that I had been given on shipboard. An empty bottle lay by him. I pushed him with my foot and he grunted.

I filled the bottle with water from the lake and emptied it on him. He immediately jumped up, gasping for air. When he saw me, he tried to strike me, but I grabbed his arm and threw him back on the ground. He demanded to know who I was. I told him that I had found his child wandering around in the bush. He told me that it was no concern of mine. I told him that I was making it my concern. I also told him that any child that wandered in the bush alone and hungry was the concern of all Indians. He told me she was not an Indian, but a half-breed and he wanted to be rid of her.

With anger, I struck him across the face and he stood up and again threatened me. I laughed at him and told him he was a poor excuse for a man. I asked him to provoke me further, so I would have an excuse to rid the world of scum. The girl came up to the lean-to and went to her father and he pushed her away. "This is the reason for all my problems," he said.

I looked at him and said, "Where were you when your woman was selling herself for a few paltry trinkets? I would hazard a guess, that you thought it was agreeable for her to do this, as long as you received part of what she earned. Now that you see the results, you refuse to accept responsibility for her and your actions. This small defenceless child is not to blame."

He looked at me closely and said, "The reason you speak as you do is because you too are a half-breed. If it is so important to you, then you take her."

I suddenly realized that I had backed myself up against a stone wall. If I accepted his offer, I would be saddled with a child I could ill afford to raise. And if I refused, I would lose face and the child would suffer his anger once I left. I could kill him, but I would still have to care for the child. I therefore had no choice but to accept the child. He was laughing at me all the while I was thinking. I lashed out in anger and hit him square in the face. He crumbled and lay still.

I went to the child and picked her up and put her on the horse and mounted behind her. She screamed, not at me, but from fear of the horse, which was the first one she had ever been close to. I calmed her down, and then headed to the north again. After she had settled down she went to sleep, because of the constant motion of the horse. She was aware that a change had come into her life and was anxious for her future.

That night by the campfire, I told her that I was taking her to a Trading Post, where a kindly woman would take care of her and that she would be safe. I tried to explain to her why there was such a quick change in her predicament. I am not sure she understood, but she seemed to accept what was happening. I gave her a wooden comb that I had from the Trading Post and she tried to comb her hair, which was a mess.

A little later she gave me back the comb with half the teeth missing. I asked her what had happened to the missing teeth and she said she didn't know. I looked at her hair and it looked no different than before. I asked her if I could cut some of it off and she agreed. I took out my sharp steel knife and cut her hair to shoulder length. There was a large pile of dirty matted hair on the ground after I had finished cutting it. It had grown down to her waist. I then took another comb and tried to comb it, but with no success.

The next morning when we were in the stream nearby, I cleaned her hair and combed it while it was wet, which made the job easier. I combed out all sorts of junk—like grass, sticks, and little creatures that I couldn't name.

She looked much better when I had finished and I am sure she felt better. It struck me that this was not a normal way for me to act. I then realized that this child was the only person I had ever felt responsible for.

When we came to a village, I traded for proper clothes for my charge and what a change they made! She really was a very attractive child, with large blue eyes that nearly filled her face. Her dark hair framed her light skin, making her look beautiful. She had nice even white teeth and a winsome smile. She was terribly underweight, but I knew that would change with proper diet.

I asked her what age she was and was surprised when she told me that she was twelve years old. Most Indian girls had matured by this age, but this girl was far from mature. At night, by the firepit, she told me as much as she could about herself. She remembered very little about her mother's family, as they would have nothing to do with her. Her father was once a very good hunter and it was not until he started to get the firewater from the trader that he started to beat her. Before that he had tried to ignore her.

Alcohol, or what the Indians called firewater, was now becoming one of the most wanted items at the Trading Posts. As if the White Man's disease was not enough to decimate the Indian culture, alcohol was used to continue the onslaught. It appeared that this drink was more potent to the Indian than to the White Man, who could drink three times more than an Indian could before he began to feel the effects. Indians reacted strangely with the first mouthful. It was the second biggest cause of the loss of the Indian's culture and lands.

I have seen Indians who were going on a peaceful visit to a neighbouring tribe start to drink, and suddenly the friendly visit would turn into a war party. They became so drunk that they were even killing each other in their stupor. In this state they would give away all they owned, causing their women and children to suffer untold grief and misery. Many of the elders tried to stop the use of alcohol and set very hard punishments for those who continued to use it, but to little avail.

The child and I still had a considerable distance to go before we arrived at the Durhams. There were many villages and Posts on the way and we were continually being invited to share firepits and hospitality. This meant we spent too much time reaching our destination. The weather was beginning to become cooler and the colours were showing in the tree leaves. I hoped that Slow Bear would be building some kind of shelter for the horses and gathering fodder for winter feed.

We were now near where the great waterfalls roared their warnings to be careful. We had passed the area where my mother had been taken by the French traders, many years before. This meant that we would be at the Trading Post within a few days. I was getting concerned that perhaps Mrs. Durham would not accept the care of the girl and I thought about what I would do in that case. I decided I would worry about that when it became necessary. Meanwhile, getting to the Trading Post was all I wanted to think about.

When we approached the Post, Slow Bear heard us coming and came out to greet us. When he saw the girl he was full of curiosity, but asked no questions. Mr. and Mrs. Durham ran to me and hugged me closely. They had waited a long time for me to get there and I was happy to be home. Peter had told them everything about me, but they showed surprise at the girl. I asked for

Peter and was told he had accepted a position with the Trading Company at the shipping docks.

We had a great homecoming and talked most of the night away. I finally told the story of the girl, who had remained silent since we had arrived. Mrs. Durham was adamant that the girl would stay with her and would hear no mention of my paying for her keep. She had always wanted a daughter and with Peter gone she needed someone to mother. Mr. Durham was also pleased with his wife's decision to keep the girl. She promptly gave her an English name, Sarah, which the girl seemed to like.

During the next few days it was apparent that Mrs. Durham and the girl were becoming fond of each other. Meanwhile, Slow Bear and I worked from morning to dark preparing a place for the horses and gathering winter food for them. The horses were feeding from a meadow nearby and getting fat from inactivity. Mr. Durham tried to ride each day, as he had done in his younger years in England. When he could leave the Post for a few hours, he went to a neighbouring Post to visit, riding one of the horses.

Finally, before the weather turned cold, we had the barn finished and, though we did not have a lot of food stored for the horses, we hoped it would last for the time we were there. We combed and brushed them every day and they became sleek and well groomed. Slow Bear and the horse he was to use became inseparable. Whenever he was nearby the horse approached him and followed him everywhere. I was happy about this relationship, because I knew he would treat the animal well.

Chapter 9
Slow Bear and I Go to Work

During this time, Slow Bear and I went over our plans to see how we were to proceed with the task facing us. It was decided that he would go ahead of me on a pre-arranged course, visiting the Trading Posts. He would look for Indians who were leaving the Post after trading there and he would check to see what they had traded and what they had received for their furs or other goods. He was to make an exact record of this transaction. I would meet him later and get this information from him before I went into that Trading Post. In the meantime, he would go on to the next Post and repeat the procedure.

We carefully mapped out the areas where we were to work and a few days later Slow Bear left. After a couple of days, I too left, following in his footsteps. Sarah cried when I took my leave, but Mrs. Durham assured her that I would return. It took most of the day to get to the nearest Trading Post, which was run by a cheerful Englishman named Mr. Boyd. I met Slow Bear the next morning at a predetermined spot, where he gave me a list of the goods that two Indians had traded and what they had received in return. Slow Bear had learned to read and write English with Mrs. Durham, but his skill still left a lot to be desired. It was a good thing that he was slow and methodical, else I would not have trusted his report.

I left him and went on to the Trading Post. Mr. Boyd examined the papers given to me by Mr. Butler, then without question handed me his books to examine. They corresponded to the lists given to me by Slow Bear and it made me happy to tell Mr. Boyd that I would send a good report to Mr. Butler. He told me that he did not agree with the Company's policy of trading liquor to the Indians. He was a particularly religious man and thought it was wrong. He did not have any liquor in his Post. I included this in my report.

After spending the night in the bush, I went on, following Slow Bear. Traveling between the Trading Posts was made much easier with the horses. I had taken my English clothes and stored them with Mrs. Durham. I really did not like the tight clothing and the three-cornered hat that was always falling off. I wore leather leggings and moccasins, short trousers, and a buckskin jacket, but no hat. In England, I had cut my hair up to my ears. Now, my hair was long and hung below my shoulders, and I tied it behind my head. Sometimes I made two braids that hung at the sides of my head.

When I again met Slow Bear, he gave me two more lists from Indians who had traded at the Post in the last two days. This Trading Post was managed by a surly Englishman named Mr. Coulter. He examined my papers very closely and, with reluctance, gave me his books. I checked them against the lists and found errors in his figures. I asked him about them and he grew quite angry, calling me a half-breed bastard and other things. I told him he could say what he wanted, but my report was going to be submitted.

This manager handled liquor. It came to him in small oaken casks, which he then put into small bottles to trade. If the Indian had enough goods to trade, he would give them the whole cask. I checked his bottles of liquor and found the liquor in them to be pretty thin, so I knew that he was diluting the rum with water, to increase his profit. When I told him what I had found he swung at me, catching me on the forehead. I backed away from him, while two Indians who were in the store at the time stood between us. He glared at us, then went into the back of the Post. After a while, he returned with a bottle of liquor and apologized to me and offered us all a drink. I refused, but the two Indians accepted quickly.

After they had left, he complained to me about how difficult it was to live so far from home. He told me that he only wanted to make enough extra money so that he could return to England. I told him that we all wanted a little extra money and I was willing to listen to any offer he cared to make. He looked at me in surprise and offered to share his bounty with me. I told him I expected half of what he made on the side and would take nothing less. Again, he reluctantly agreed. I told him that the payments would start that day and he had no choice but to give me some of his ill-gotten funds.

I felt no remorse about doing this. I believed that this was one way that I could take advantage of the White Man. I had spent three years of my life learning business practise and if this was the way White men practised business, then I had not wasted my three years. Since the White Man had come to our country, they had not done business in an honest manner. They made agreements that they did not honor; they took land that was not theirs; they used our women, although many had women at home. Their justice system was different from the Indians'. They made laws for the White Man and different laws for Indians. It was perfectly all right for a White man to steal from an Indian but not for the Indian to steal from the White man.

During the next four months, Slow Bear and I worked the territory of the Seneca and the Delaware. On the average, there was one honest trader in six. Most of the thefts were of a minor nature, usually against the Indians. To the White Man, this was acceptable, but not to me. Besides my pay from the Trading Company, I now had a good income from the dishonest traders. The dishonesty

I found was mostly in watered-down liquor. But it seemed that no matter how weak the liquor, the Indians kept trading for it and getting just as drunk.

I had to make many trips to the Durham Post to hide my money, because it was too dangerous to carry it around. I buried it in a place known only to myself, keeping just enough cash on me to do business with. The Durhams were always glad to see me and I them. The girl named Sarah by the Durhams was getting some flesh on her. She was beginning to look more like a girl of twelve years, though she was not as filled-out as were most Indian girls of that age. It struck me that she was only eight years younger than I. I considered her a child and she considered me to be an adult.

Slow Bear and I were working in the Cayuga area when we began to have a few problems. Traders were giving me trouble. I was even attacked by some Indians that they had hired to kill me. Slow Bear seemed to have a sixth sense, knowing when trouble would be coming and had managed to thwart the trader's plans. I decided to fight back. Slow Bear hired a group of Indians who were willing to help us.

One trader who was particularly troublesome was picked as our target. Slow Bear and his friends met with me in the bush, near the Trading Post, and I told them the plan. We were to disguise ourselves as another Indian tribe that were usually with the French. I was to dress as a French trader and we were to raid the English Trading Post, which continually happened in this area. We were to speak only in French, or in an Indian dialect that the trader would not recognize and then only when necessary. I was to do most of the talking in French. My Indian friends were to split the Trading Post's trade goods amongst them, while I would get all the furs. These furs were usually marked by the traders with their Post's number so they could be traced, but I had friends that would accept them.

We attacked the next evening and the trader was caught unprepared for us. It was easy to take control of him and his family. There were no other Indians around that were friendly to him, so we had our own way. We then let him pack a few belongings and leave.

He was so eager to go that he didn't object. He had expected us to kill him and his wife, which so often happened in similar raids between the French and the English traders. One of our group followed him for the next few days to make sure that he made no effort to return to the Post.

In the meantime, the Indians looted the store of all the trade goods and most got drunk on the liquor that was taken. Slow Bear and I packed the furs into bundles and had two of the most trusted of the Indians help us move them. We burned the Post to the ground and left the other Indians drinking and enjoying themselves. It took us three days to get to a friend of mine, who gladly took the furs off my hands and paid me in cash for them. Fur trading was becoming difficult because the fur animals had been over-hunted and the number of hunters were continually increasing. The fact that White men were settling on some of the prime hunting areas was not helping the situation. They would hunt, too, so the Indians had more competition.

Mr. Butler himself was working the area to our south, and we would meet once in a while in a prearranged place to compare notes. He appeared to be more than satisfied with my work and praised me for getting Slow Bear to help. He said that the French to the west were getting bolder and bolder. He asked me to go there to take a look, and to see what could be done to protect the English traders from the French.

Chapter 10
The Mohawk, My Father's Tribe

Slow Bear and I went east to the Mohawk territory, passing many English Trading Posts. We stayed with other tribes of the Iroquois and were welcomed. There were several White settlements here, but most of them were to the south, by the salt water.

Two Faces and Slow Bear

We were to report to an English Army outpost in the area of Mohawk Lake. Before we arrived, we spent some time with the Mohawk. The Indian people did not like the English Army, who were inclined to be both demanding and arrogant toward them.

We went directly to the Army camp and reported to the officer in charge, a sergeant called Michael Stone-Heming. He was a big, rough-talking man, using many curse words to punctuate his language. He was a very arrogant person and let Slow Bear and me know in no uncertain terms who the boss was. I let him talk, politely listening to his barrage of words.

When he was finished, I nodded to Slow Bear and stood up to leave. The Sergeant asked me where I thought I was going. I told him that I didn't work for the Army and had no intention of ever taking orders from him in my own country, which was called Kanata by the Iroquois. He blustered for a moment, then said he did not want to give the impression that I was to work for him; nevertheless, that is what he had said.

I then made it plain to him that I would recruit a group of my fellow natives. We would go in advance of the English and do the actual raiding of the French Trading Posts. In this way, it would look as if the English were not involved with these raids. For this, we wanted to have the furs that were taken in such raids. The Sergeant insisted that the Army get the trade goods.

After much haggling, it was agreed. We, the Indians, would lay out the direction and the Trading Posts that were to be raided. The furs were to be shared among the Indians and the trade goods would go to the Army. It would be left to the Indians if the French trader and his family were to be killed or let go, depending on their resistance. The Indians were to supply the food for the Army on the trail when possible, but the Army was not to rely continually on the Indians for food. The Army was to supply us with two rifles and ammunition.

Slow Bear and I had a meal with the Army, then took our horses and the two new rifles that we had been given and went on to the nearest Indian village. Here we had no problem recruiting fifteen good men to accompany us. They agreed to the terms negotiated by us with the English Army, although they did not particularly like the idea of having to supply the food for everyone. We immediately laid out our plans and the place where we would strike first.

After a few days, we left for the northwest, going toward the fresh-water lake. This was known to be a place where several French Trading Posts did business. Within three days we attacked our first Post which was situated by the shoreline. Slow Bear had surveyed the place with another Indian for a full day. It was not the busiest time of the year for them, as most of the pelts had been brought in. The Post was manned by an older Frenchman and his wife. They offered no resistance and showed surprise that they were being attacked. It was known that there were many French Posts nearby, so they had felt secure.

We let them go. We did not feel comfortable in injuring them. They appreciated our not killing them and left quickly with a few belongings. One of our people went with them, to make sure that they left the area. We quickly bundled all the furs and packed the trading goods for the Army. The Army people arrived about three hours after we had finished packing everything.

Sergeant Heming looked over their share of the goods that we had taken and said he thought that they should get part of the furs. I let him know in no uncertain terms that this was our agreement and it would not be changed. I began to realize that I disliked this man immensely. This feeling was shared by my Indian friends. I had already taken the precaution of having the furs taken by some of my men to a Trading Post to the south. I had also made arrangements with a tribe of Mohawk to store the furs for me, if need be.

We wasted no time eating the food left by the French. We then burned the Post to the ground. The Indians that lived near the Post were curious, but showed no interest after they were given some trinkets from the Post. They were Mohawk and had no personal interest in the French. After discussing plans, we left the Army and went along the coast to the east. After four days we came in sight of the Post that we were seeking.

Chapter 11
Problems

Slow Bear and another Indian began their surveillance of the next Post, while the rest of us scouted the surrounding area. Aside from a few Mohawk families, there were no other people. The next day, early in the morning, we attacked the Post. The Post manager was up, but his wife and child were still in bed. It was over quickly, as we had taken them entirely by surprise.

The Post manager was about thirty years old; his wife was a little younger. When they pulled her from bed, she lost her nightwear and stood there naked. She was a nice-looking woman and some of the Indians wanted to use her, but I made it clear that she was to be treated with respect. I spoke to her and her man, telling them that we would not hurt them if they cooperated.

This, they realized, they could not refuse to do. They packed what they could carry of their own things and left, accompanied by one of the Indians to make sure that they kept going. Again we bundled the furs and I sent them away before the Army showed up. Some of our men got into the liquor and were very drunk by the time the Army arrived. Sergeant Heming was furious with me for not waiting for him to check the furs and for letting the Indians consume his liquor.

By now, I had enough of this blustering bully, so I turned on him in like fury. I told him that if he didn't like the way we handled things, to raid the French Trading Posts himself. I stalked away from him and went into the forest. The next morning, a soldier came to my camp with an apology from the Sergeant, who said that I was to carry on. I talked it over with the other Indians and they agreed to continue, but only if the Army stood by when we raided the Posts.

This meant that the Army had to travel with us but stay hidden while the Indians did the actual raiding. Some of the soldiers wanted to disguise themselves as Indians and join us. We picked the soldiers that would be easy to disguise and they came with us. The next Post was in a more crowded area, near a White Man's village, so we needed all the help we could get.

After a week's traveling, we arrived near the Post. It was beside a river which flowed into a lake about two miles away. The White Man's village was at the mouth of this river. We planned our attack very carefully. Slow Bear and two other Indians were to get all the information they could on the Post, while other Indians were to go to local tribes and arrange for them to be away when we attacked.

Some of these tribal leaders wanted to share in the goods, so we made arrangements. They wanted mostly blankets and knives. The Sergeant and I came to an agreement, so that we both gave up the same value of goods.

About four days later we attacked the Post. They must have been expecting us, because there was much resistance. Some of the people had come from the White Man's village to help the Post manager. They expected only Indians, but surrendered when the soldiers opened fire from the surrounding trees. They had not seen the soldiers, but thought there were more Indians in the bush. We had lost several Indians and some were wounded. About three White men had been killed.

There were five White men left alive and two of them were wounded. My Indian friends wanted to finish off the whole five of them, but I said they had surrendered, so they could live. They still did not agree with me, as they knew that the White Man did not accept surrender from us. I had to give them all a better share of the furs to quiet them down and agree to accept my decision. Sergeant Heming heard of my problems and for once he agreed with me.

We quickly packed everything necessary and made the White men carry some of the bundles of furs. Soon the Post was burning and we made haste to leave. Some reinforcements were coming from the village and we did not want to waste time fighting them. We headed south and after a half day's walking, we released the White men and continued going south. That night, we made no campfire, in case we were still being pursued. We had meals of dried meat, which the Army men hated and grumbled loudly about.

We left the Army the next morning and headed northwest, where we knew there was a French Trading Post. The Army had made arrangements to meet us nearby. That afternoon, after we climbed a small hill, a shot rang out and one of our people fell to the ground. We all went scrambling down the hill again and gathered at the bottom. I split the group into two and had each one go a different way around the hill. Soon I could make out a man, sitting on the hill, about three hundred feet away.

I signaled to Slow Bear, who then saw him too. We crept quietly through the underbrush until he was in range of our guns. Slowly, Slow Bear took careful aim, then fired. The man stood for a moment, as though suspended, and then crashed down the hillside. In the meantime, the other half of our group had come up behind the other men and soon had them under control. When we were together again, it was obvious to us that these men had followed us from the Post.

There had been five of them, and two were dead. We now had three prisoners. This time I had no control over my Indian friends whatsoever. They intended to kill them and that was that. But first, they intended to make them pay for killing one of their friends. This meant that they would be tortured.

I would have nothing to do with this, so I left the camp and went to the forest by myself. Later, Slow Bear found me and told me that the White men had been skinned and would soon die.

When morning came, I went to the camp. The White men were still tied to posts by the firepit, but were dead. The Indians piled firewood around them and burned them where they were. They buried the other two where they had fallen. I had seen what White men had done to Indians and what they had done to other White men. I had no wish to do anything like this to any man, whoever he was. But both the Indian and the White Man knew what to expect if taken alive.

We had a ceremony for the Indian who had been killed and by the time we were finished, the Army had arrived. Sergeant Heming said nothing when he heard that my Indian friends had tortured and killed the prisoners. He felt that the French had wanted to fight, so therefore had to take the consequences if they lost. We now had to plan the next assault. This was one of the biggest Posts in the territory so we had to use caution.

My Indian friends made a good meal of venison and greens and it was one of the better meals so far. The Sergeant complained that the Indians who had been left with him to supply food were too lazy. It was then decided that from now on we would all travel together, but the Army would still keep a low profile.

It took five days to finish the investigation into the Post's defence and we were surprised to see that they were very lax. It was decided that we would attack the next day at the meal time of the Post personnel. This, we hoped, would catch them unawares. So far we had always attacked at daybreak, so this would be different.

The next morning, we prepared for the attack, positioning all where they were needed. Slow Bear and three other Indians went inside the Post, making it look as though they had furs to trade.

When they had the attention of the traders, we charged in, making loud noises to make them think our group was larger than it was. Most of the French gave up without a struggle, but one man ran to the small church nearby and sounded the bells, letting people in the village know what was happening.

We quickly tied up the prisoners and made haste to gather all the furs we could. The Army people grabbed what they wanted and we left hurriedly. We could hear the townspeople coming to help the trader. We went into the forest, following what game trails presented themselves. The Indians could make better time than the Army people, making it necessary for us to slow down so they could keep up with us.

We knew we were being followed, so we did not stop until the next morning. We left a group of Indians to keep watch on our trail, and the rest of us tried to get some rest. About two hours later our guards came to tell us the French were nearby and that we had better leave. I asked how many were in their group and they said they estimated about twenty men. I felt it best to move on, but the Sergeant wanted to set a trap for them. I told him that this terrain was not the best place to ambush anyone and asked him to reconsider.

After some pondering and advice from his men, he agreed to go on and ambush them later at a more appropriate spot. We traveled on, with the French in pursuit, until we came to a small Indian village between high hills. Slow Bear talked with the Chief of the tribe and enlisted his help. We spent the remainder of the day preparing the ambush, keeping the French under surveillance at the same time.

The next day the French arrived at our ambush and because of the added assistance of the local Indians, we killed most and took a few prisoners. The French seemed to consider that this was their territory and the English did not have a right here. The Sergeant and the prisoners argued about this, until I told them both that this was Indian land and they were in an Indian village.

They chose to ignore me, so I let them go on arguing. The Indians wanted to torture and kill the French, so I had to negotiate them out of it. We let them keep all the possessions of the French except the guns, which Slow Bear and I made disappear for our own use later. The Sergeant asked about them, but did not push the subject. We learned from the prisoners that the French were putting soldiers into the area, to protect their Trading Posts and villages.

We had already become aware of this from other sources, so we were not surprised. The Sergeant had requested additional troops from his superior and I had recruited about fifty Indians for this eventuality. We now knew that this was full warfare between the English and the French. We were aware also that the homelands of the French and English were at that time preparing for war between their countries as well.

My agreement with the English was now redundant, because we would be fighting anyplace and anywhere, so there would not be goods from Trading Posts to share. It was now the victor take the spoils. The only thing left of our agreement was that the Indians were to hunt and feed the whole group. My friends did not like this arrangement and it was not long before they found a way to change it.

After a particularly brutal battle with the French, where most of the enemy had been killed as well as several of our men, my Indian friends made the evening meal, as had been the custom. It was usually a stew, made of what vegetation they could gather plus meat, usually venison, which had been hunted and killed that day. When the meal was prepared, everyone gathered with his board or bowl to be served.

The soldiers pushed to the front of the line as usual and, as was usual, there was no objection from the Indians, since they knew that the first served did not get as much solid food, but more liquid. By waiting, they got the more solid food at the bottom of the pot. But this night, the English suddenly dropped their bowls and headed into the brush, where we could hear them retching and vomiting. I quickly went to see the cause and looking into the cooking pot, could see feet, hands, and various other parts of a human body floating around.

I felt like joining the others in the brush, but at that time the Sergeant appeared. He looked into the pot and turned a pasty pale colour. "What is the meaning of this?" he wanted to know.

"Is there some kind of a problem?" asked one of the Indians.

"You damn well know what I mean!" screamed the Sergeant. "You have put human meat into the stew! Do you think we are cannibals?"

"I can't understand," the Indian replied. "This is the same as we have eaten the past two nights and you did not complain before."

The Sergeant looked at the stew again, then he made a beeline for the brush.

The Indian grinned from ear to ear and gave me a look that told me everything. I later learned that they had put body parts of a dead Frenchman into the stew to force the English to provide and prepare their own meals. It worked. The English never ate with us again. They thought us all savages and cannibals. The truth was it sickened us too, and we never used that cooking pot again.

Chapter 12
We Attack a Village

Our next encounter with the French happened the following week. It was in a village surrounded by a high palisade. We knew that it was inhabited by about a hundred French families. They had gardens surrounding their village; consequently there was no cover for us so that we could approach without being shot at. We made plans while keeping the inhabitants under siege. No one entered or left the village. A group of Indians from a nearby village asked if they could join us. They were angry because the French had taken their land and abused their women.

I accepted their offer without discussion with the English. It was decided that we would attack after dark when there was no moon. We waited for three days and there was no movement in the village. We knew they were preparing for our assault. In the meantime we spent our time making torches of pine pitch and gathering dry brush to stack against the palisade gates.

On the night we attacked, the sky was black. Silently, the Indians piled the brush against the wall by the gate and, when all was ready, threw lighted pitch torches into the brush. The defenders poured water down onto the fire, but our arrows rained up at them, driving them from the wall. Soon, the palisade was burning, even though the defenders wet the inside of the wall. The Indians kept starting fires along the wall from place to place, making the work of the French scattered and ineffectual.

The soldiers then stormed the gate with axes, while their comrades fired bullets into the cracks in the walls.

The defenders tried to mount a defence, but they were overwhelmed by our numbers.

Finally we broke through, and the soldiers went through the gates firing their guns at the people inside. After half an hour the French called for surrender. Quickly we gathered all the men together and put them into one building, which was the church. The priest begged for mercy, but one of the Indians shoved a knife into his throat. I asked them for control, but the Indian involved was from the nearby village and had a score to settle with these people.

We put the women and children into two nearby buildings, then looked over the rest of the place. In one small building we found eight young Indian girls, who, we were to learn, were abused by the Frenchmen and made to work like slaves by the women. This made the Indians very angry and I could see that we were in for trouble.

I asked the Chiefs to calm the men, then I went to talk with the Sergeant. He told me that any Indian not obeying his orders would be shot. I told him that he had better look to his own back and walked away.

I talked with the Chiefs and Shaman. They told me they had tried to keep order with the Indians, but things were getting out of hand. There were some thirty-odd White men and about a hundred and fifty Indians that were still alive after the battle. The next morning the soldiers took some of the French prisoners and had them bury the dead—theirs and ours. The Indians took care of their own dead, according to tradition. I could feel that the mood was very volatile, so I went into a building away from the rest of the people, taking Slow Bear with me.

About midnight, we were awakened by six Indians entering the building. They seized Slow Bear and me and bound us tightly. They said they had no desire to harm us and only wanted to make sure we would sound no alarm to the White men. We were then left with two

Indians guarding us. Later, we heard shouts and a few shots, then more screams of anger. Before daylight, some Indians came in and, taking Slow Bear and me, went to the building housing the White men.

We entered and were surprised to see that the White men were being held as prisoners. The Indians then cut us loose and told us they intended to make us stay with the White men as prisoners also. We objected, but to no avail. They then went out, leaving us facing the White people. The Sergeant called to me and asked what was going on. We discussed our predicament and could find no reason for our captivity, except that the Indians were dissatisfied with us.

We could hear the shouts of the Indians, who by this time had indulged in the White Man's liquor. There were screams from men being tortured and cries from women. We were to learn later that the Indians had gone on a drunken rampage, torturing the men and raping the White women. They made the Indian captive women help with the tortures and the rapes. They were, in their own minds, exacting revenge. The Sergeant asked if there was anything I could do. I replied that it was too late and that we had better think of our own hides.

Slow Bear and I looked over the building. We could see that the only escape possible was through the chimney hole in the roof. So we busied ourselves building a pole ladder of sorts, to get to the rafters and then the roof. Some of the soldiers helped, but most of them just sat and complained about our predicament. Some even made hostile motions toward Slow Bear and me. The Sergeant kept them under control.

Things began to quiet down before morning. Slow Bear and I climbed up onto the roof. Lying there quietly, we could observe most of the village. We could see that two poles had been put into the ground and Frenchmen were tied to them. Around them on the ground were the bodies of earlier victims. We could see the naked bodies of French women, lying were they had been raped and killed. Some, still living, were trying to crawl away into the shadows. There were some Indians sitting with their backs to walls, cradling bottles in their arms.

We knew there were guards below us, watching the White men. They too had been drinking and were discussing how they would kill the soldiers. Slow Bear had crept above them and motioned me to follow. Below, I could make out two Indians standing with their backs to the wall, while another sat in a drunken stupor. Slow Bear nodded to me and we both dropped to the ground in front of the two that were standing. Slow Bear produced a knife, from I don't know where, and quickly dispatched the one by him. I had seized the one in front of me and had stopped him from making a sound by holding him by the neck. Slow Bear quickly cut his throat. The drunken one that was sitting just stared at us. I kicked him in the head and he lay unconscious.

We made a quick survey, then returned and opened the door of our recent prison. With Slow Bear by the door, I went in and spoke quietly with the Sergeant. I told him that if he valued his life, he was to do as I said. He agreed and soon the soldiers were making their way out of the village, as Slow Bear took care of the guard by the gate. We quickly made for a creek nearby and then followed it downstream.

Chapter 13
Escape

When we had reached the lake that the stream flowed into, we decided that our group of Indians and the White people should separate. The Whites went west and my party went to the east. We had the more dangerous route, going deeper into French territory, but we knew the Indians were friendly to us and would hide us from the French if they should pursue us.

As we went easterly, the Indians that we met told us the French had Army personnel looking for the English in their territory. They had been told that the English and French were close to having a war in their homelands. We had been aware of this and were quick to side with the English. Most of the Iroquois Nation did also. Some of the tribes that lived closer to the largest French village near Hochalaga sided with the French. It was their mistake.

We decided to go in a southerly direction. We learned later that we were none too soon, as the French had been waiting for us further east. The woods were now full of camps of both English soldiers and Indians. We avoided them when we could. When it was unavoidable, we would be questioned for hours on end, since they wanted as much information on the French as we could provide.

We would often tell them where we would go if we were in their position, but we never knew if they accepted our advice or not. Some of the Indians that were with us joined the soldiers, but most of them just wanted to go home. Slow Bear and I, along with two other trusted friends, separated from the others and made our way to the English Post where our looted furs had been taken.

The Post looked deserted when we arrived, but we found the trader nearby. He told us that he had waited for us to come. He had closed the Post because he feared that the French were around. A Post about two days' journey from his had been raided and burned. He had moved everything out to the larger village to the south. Our furs had been traded for cash as we had requested, and the money was placed safely in that village.

He finished what he had returned to do, then we left, going toward the village to the south. It took us five days, but long before we reached the village we could hear gunfire. When we climbed a ridge above the village, we could see that there was a siege going on. A group of French soldiers surrounded the palisades of the village and were firing on the inhabitants, who were returning the fire.

We realized that we could do nothing to help them, for there were only eight of us: Slow Bear, our two Indian friends, the trader, his three Indian employees, and I. Slow Bear and another Indian volunteered to go to the nearest Indian camp to try to get help. This was a two-day journey, so they could not return for at least four days. I wondered if the village could hold out that long, but we had no other choice.

After Slow Bear and his companion had left, the rest of us settled down for a long wait. For two days we sat idly by and watched what was going on below. We kept hidden from sight, but could still see everything from our vantage point. There were about thirty-five French soldiers involved, against a village of some hundred people, most of whom were women and children.

It soon became apparent that the village was weakening. The French were hitting it from all sides, but the shooting from the village was getting sparse, so it was obvious that they were saving ammunition. It was decided amongst us that we could help them from our vantage point. Even if the French turned their attention to us, we could escape into the woods behind us. The fact that the trader's wife and children were within the village made us act.

Fate then took a hand. Fortunately for us, a group of Indians appeared just before we took any action. They had been hunting nearby, when Slow Bear met them and had asked for their help. The White people's village was known to them, so they agreed to help us. They numbered twenty men, but they had only three rifles among them. Because of the surrounding forest, they hoped that they would be able to get close enough to use bows and arrows.

We spread out about two hundred feet apart, then started firing down on the French. We made as much noise as possible, to make out that we were a large party. The French were at first surprised and then, knowing our position, grouped on the opposite side of the village, protected from our fire by the palisade. We could hear cheers from inside the village, and they then increased their fire on the French.

Suddenly, everything was quiet. The French had withdrawn into the trees, to avoid the fire from the village. We knew they would regroup close to the gate in order to try to keep us out of the village. It was a waste of their time, as we did not intend to become trapped inside. We sent two Indians down the ridge to watch for any French that were trying to approach us from behind.

One of the Indians returned to say that the French had regrouped in the woods near the village gate. This is what we were waiting for, because we knew they would be no match for us in the forest. I led half of our men down one side of the ridge to where the French were positioned; the trader and his men went down the other. One of my men went ahead, then soon returned to say that the French were in a small clearing ahead. Very slowly, we crept close enough to see and hear them.

They were cleaning guns and preparing to climb the hill that we had just left. I spread the men in a circle around them and on a signal, we all opened fire at the same time. The trader did the same. We then melted into the forest as quickly and quietly as we could. I could see that six of the French had fallen from our fire.

We again climbed about halfway to the ridge and spaced ourselves out, waiting for the French to pursue us. We stayed hidden for over three hours. Suddenly a lone Frenchman appeared, looking carefully for signs of us. No one made a move. Then the Frenchman disappeared as quickly as he had appeared. We patiently waited, knowing he would lead them to us.

The trader indicated to me that he was going to go higher up the ridge, taking ten men with him. I waved agreement and he melted silently away. A few minutes later, five Frenchmen appeared, looking about cautiously. I signaled to my men and we all opened fire together, felling three of them. The other two turned and ran, but three of my men followed and soon caught up to them and killed them.

When my group was finally together, and after we had picked up the arms of the dead Frenchmen, we carefully, slowly followed to where the trader had gone. Before we reached the top of the ridge, I took my group around to the other side, approaching from that direction. It was a wise decision, as we came up behind a group of the French that were about to attack the trader and his men on the top of the ridge.

I spread my group out, telling them to wait for the French or the trader to begin firing. An Indian who was with the trader appeared on the ridge. The French fired at him and soon both the trader and his group and the French began shooting. My group started to fire up at the French. This crossfire went on for a while. The French knew that they were caught between two groups, and tried to fight both ways, in vain.

Soon, the French held up a white cloth, so we took them prisoners. There were eight in this group, four of whom had slight wounds. We marched them to the ridge where the trader waited.

The prisoners showed surprise to see that we numbered so few. They asked where our main group was. We told them that we were all there was and they stared in disbelief. I told the leader not to forget that we had the men in the village. I told him that we were more experienced and more at home in the forest than they were.

The trader, the other Indians, and I made a decision to take the leader of our captives to speak to his commander in an effort to persuade them to surrender. We warned him that if they did not, we would kill them all. I reminded him that we were born in the forest and knew how to fight there to best advantage.

The next morning, after a hasty meal, we went down the hill to the French camp. Our captives remained quiet, on threat of instant death. Leaving them bound and guarded by one man, we took the leader with us. After we had lain hidden from the view of the French for a while, I had one Indian, who was an accurate bowman, fire an arrow into the ground by the leader's feet.

They immediately went for their arms, but I called out for them to relax, as we would not fight as yet. The Frenchman we had as prisoner was untied and he walked into their camp. He went straight up to his leader and I could see a small group surround him. They seemed to talk for some time, then the leader called for me to come and discuss terms. I called back that I refused, unless the head man of the village was included in the discussion.

This was arranged and he gave permission for one of my men to go to the village. I spoke to the trader, so he went around the French and entered the gate of the village, after identifying himself. Soon he and another man emerged from the village and joined us. The man showed his appreciation for our intervention in his problem. He and all my men held a meeting and arranged the terms of the French surrender.

Just in time, Slow Bear arrived with about twenty Indians from the nearby village. With these reinforcements, we were able to strengthen our hand. I called to the French leader, requesting a conference and he agreed.

He, two of his men, Slow Bear, the man from the village and I met in a clearing, away from the rest. I told him that our terms were that they should lay down their arms and leave this area. We would help to treat their wounded. Any damage done to the village, they would have to repair. We agreed that no harm would come to them if they complied.

The French withdrew to consider our offer. After an hour, they returned to say that they would accept the terms. My Indian friends gathered their arms together and we all went into the village. The White people looked in amazement to see that a small group of Indians had helped them against the French. I cannot say that they did not show their appreciation, but it struck me and my Indian friends that they trusted the French more than they did us. Perhaps I was being unfair, but it was evident that they treated the French with more respect. For instance, the French got fed before we did.

We stayed with this village for four more days, but not within the palisade, as we did not trust the White people any more than they trusted us. The Frenchmen repaired the damage they had done to the village and we then let them leave. We had taken care of their wounded and given them enough provisions to last until they got to their own village. The French leader and I had time to talk considerably, and I was surprised at the intelligence of the man. He really did not like the country and wanted to return to France as soon as he could, because he missed his family and friends.

The people in the village wasted no time in getting back to normal. The men were soon in the fields, harvesting their crops. The trader found that his wife and family had suffered no injuries and as for me, I soon had my money. After we had settled accounts, Slow Bear and I were ready to leave. Our two friends wanted to stay another day, so we left them. The Indians from the village nearby left, happy that things had turned out well.

Chapter 14
We Go Home

Slow Bear and I both wanted to go home for a while—
he to the village of our mother and her family and I to
the Durhams' Trading Post. I had a considerable amount
of money on my person, so I wanted to put it where I
considered it would be safe. I had buried money there
before.

We traveled together for a week or so, then Slow
Bear left me to go his way. I still had two weeks of
travel ahead. I often wondered how I had managed without the horse. But even on horseback, it was a long trip.
I was not comfortable with the money in the saddle bags.
There were many White people around the forest and I
had to pass a number of White settlements on my way.

These settlements were usually close to where there
had been a Trading Post, or near an Indian village. I
assumed they felt that if the area was good enough for
Indians to have a village, it would be good for them.
They were, of course, right. The Indian didn't put a village just anywhere. The area had to have sufficient game
and good enough soil to raise crops for food. The village
was always near a good supply of water and in a place
that was protected from prevailing winds and the drifting
of deep snow.

For the most part, I was welcomed at these settlements.
They could see that I was a half-breed and posed no
threat to them. I went to the Indian villages whenever
it was possible, because they made me more welcome
and I enjoyed listening to the stories by their campfires.
In turn, I always had stories to tell them.

As I came closer to the Trading Post, I was tired and grew careless. This was foolish of me. One day when I was letting the horse walk slowly in a grove of maple trees, I dozed in the saddle. Suddenly, I was knocked from the horse and struck my head on a nearby tree. I was out cold. When I regained consciousness, I found that I was bound hand and foot. I was also blindfolded, so I could not see.

A voice said, "So, half-breed, you are awake."

I could not tell by the voice who it could be. It sounded like a very young person who spoke Iroquois fluently.

"I am awake, no thanks to you," I replied. "Who are you that you would attack me in such a cowardly way?"

"I am no coward," the voice replied. "Do not blame me because you are stupid enough to sleep while riding a horse with saddle bags full of gold pieces."

"So you are just a thief," I taunted, "as well as a coward, else why would you blindfold me?"

"I will remove your blindfold, stupid one."

The blindfold was torn from my head and the sunlight blinded me for an instant. Before me was a very slender person dressed in Indian clothes. I saw that it was a woman and my surprise made the person laugh.

I asked, "Who in the world are you? Where is your accomplice?"

She chuckled. "I have no need for an accomplice, and you have been away so long you do not recognize me. I am Sarah."

I stared for a moment, then I realized that this was the half-breed girl I had left with the Durhams a very long time ago.

"You seem surprised that I have grown up," she said. "Do you think time stands still for everyone when you are not here?"

She cut my bonds and I sat up, rubbing my head. She told me that I had suffered no lasting injury and that my baggage was still on the horse. I looked at her and asked why she attacked me. She said she attacked every man in the forest before they attacked her. It made no difference whether they were Indian or White, they all wanted to take advantage of a woman alone in the forest.

My head ached, but it was really my pride that suffered. I was stupid to think I was so safe that I could fall asleep on the horse. This was a lesson well-deserved. I looked at her closely and could see a girl who still had the biggest eyes and skin that was clear as water. Her hair was black and tied behind her head. She had a band around her head. She was wearing Indian clothes which were men's—a shirt, pants, and leggings with high moccasins made of buckskin. She was slim and around five feet tall.

Suddenly she said, "If you are finished gawking, we can get on to the Trading Post."

I got up, went to the horse, and mounted, not saying a word. She quickly jumped up onto the horse in front of me. It happened so fast there was no time to object. I took the reins and had the horse walk slowly along a game trail until we hit a narrow road leading to the Post.

I could feel her body and it was hard and lean. She was an active person, else how could she have jumped onto the horse in front of me so quickly with no apparent effort?

We said nothing and soon I could tell that she was dozing, which was easy to do with the motion of the horse. I imagined also that she felt secure with me. She kept waking with a start and then would doze again. We traveled along like this for about four hours and were now nearing the Post. I traveled alongside a stream that ran past the Post and watched for a certain area that I knew of. Here, the trail ran along a steep bank which dropped down into the stream. At this spot, there was a deep pool.

Slow Bear and I had used this pool for swimming many years ago. We had been able to dive from the bank into the water. As we came near the spot, I slowed the horse down. When we were at the top of the bank, I seized Sarah's left leg and threw her into the pool. She shouted in surprise and when she hit the water I put the horse into a fast gallop. I could hear her saying things that I would not repeat.

Chapter 15
With Sarah and the Durhams

Slow Bear was coming from the Post, having heard the hollering going on. I told him what had happened. He laughed and told me that I had better keep on riding. I removed the saddle bags and he took the horse. I then went into the Post. The Durhams were happy to see me again and both talked at once. We were sitting at their kitchen table when I heard someone come in the back door. I knew it was Sarah, because wet buckskin makes a distinctive noise when one walks. She went directly to her room and both the Durhams smiled, for they knew what had happened.

I was told that Peter was doing well in the head office of the Trading Company and that he had returned home several times. Mrs. Durham started to make the evening meal, so her husband and I went to the stable that Slow Bear and I had made for the two horses. It was made of posts, with one door in the end large enough for the horses to enter.

We had built it against a bank so it did not need a wall at the back. The roof was level with the top of the bank, which made it possible to walk onto the roof from there. It was made of poles, which we covered with earth and grass. It sloped away from the bank for drainage. Inside the barn there were two stalls at the front end near the doorway. At the other end there was a room with one window. There was a space for storing food for the horses between the room and the stalls.

The nearby stream flowed by one side of the barn, so one could water the horses there. Slow Bear had made the room livable by putting in a floor of planks and poles on the side of the bank so as to cover it. This made a comfortable room for him and me to sleep in. There were only two bedrooms in the back of the Trading Post—one for the Durhams and the one Peter had used that was now Sarah's.

Slow Bear and I moved my luggage into this room and then I helped him brush down the horses. By the time we were finished, Mrs. Durham called to us. The kitchen table had been set and we sat down to eat. At this time Sarah entered from her room and I was surprised to see that she now wore a White woman's dress. It was printed all over with pink flowers and went down to the floor. It was gathered at the waist and had short puffy sleeves. The neckline was cut across and it looked like her breasts were ready to pop out. She had combed her hair down each side of her face. With the black hair and large blue eyes against her pale skin, she was absolutely beautiful.

I stood up when she entered the room and held her chair for her when she sat down. She acted as though I was doing what she expected. The Durhams smiled and Slow Bear just grunted a greeting. She kept her eyes down and showed no emotions whatsoever. I wondered if she was mad at me for dumping her into the water. I had no doubt that I would soon find out.

The next morning at dawn I took my saddle bags of gold coins to my hiding place to put with the rest of the money for safe-keeping. I removed the flat rock and was astounded to find my coins gone. Since this was a well-hidden place, I couldn't believe that someone had just stumbled onto them. I found another spot to hide the saddle bags and went to the Trading Post. Mrs. Durham had made a light meal for us, so while we were all together, I asked if any strangers had been around the Post. When they assured me that no one had been there, I told them about my missing coins. They all showed surprise that they had disappeared, but could not help me.

Later that day, when Slow Bear and I were walking along the stream, he suggested that the only one who could have taken the coins was Sarah. I did not accept this, but he added that the Durhams were much too honest to take my coins. I thought about this and asked him what he would suggest we do. He said he would follow her wherever she went and hopefully she would lead him to where she had hidden the coins. I agreed to give it a try. For the next few days she did not move without Slow Bear behind her, watching her every move.

I found that all three places where I had hidden coins had been robbed. Every cent I had was gone. To say that I was angry was understating how I felt. About ten days went by. Then one night Slow Bear told me he had found where Sarah spent a lot of her time. He wondered if she would have a secret place nearby. He had observed her sitting on a rock above a small, narrow ravine which was filled with huge boulders.

The next day, using the pretext that we were going to give the horses needed exercise, we saddled up and left the Post. We went in the opposite direction from where we intended to travel, then circled around to the ravine that Sarah had gone to. Slow Bear showed me where she had sat on a particular rock. He then hid the horses and stood guard out of sight while I went into the ravine. It was very hard climbing. It was made worse because I had no idea what I was looking for.

I spent three hours climbing over and under boulders. Just when I was about to give up, a rabbit jumped up in front of me, then disappeared into a small crevice that was overhung by a stone wall. I knelt down and could see a small opening.

I crawled up into this opening with very little space to spare. I could barely make out a small room. It was about three feet high and about six feet by five feet in size. The floor was sand and I could see rabbit droppings along with other debris. Back against one wall and very hard to see, I could make out the canvas bags that held my money.

The space was too narrow for me to proceed, so I backed out and went to find Slow Bear. I told him what I had found. He was glad that he had been proven right. Now, we had to decide what we should do. It was decided that we would follow her to the crevice and face her with our knowledge at that time. For the next few days Slow Bear and I kept a sharp watch on Sarah. Eventually, she went to the ravine. We followed her but not too closely, and when she disappeared into the ravine we were right behind her.

I watched as Sarah crawled into the crevice, then we rushed over there. We blocked off the entrance with huge boulders. We could hear her cursing and asking what we were up to. We made no answer. When she was securely blocked in the crevice, we left. When we arrived back at the Post, we told the Durhams what we had done. While Mr. Durham thought it was "just punishment," Mrs. Durham did not, and insisted that we go and release her. I told Slow Bear that I would return and release her. Taking one of the horses, I went to the ravine.

I went to the crevice and could hear nothing. I started to remove the stones blocking the entrance. When they were all removed, I called to Sarah. I did not get a reply, so I bent over to look into the cave and I was knocked unconscious with a blow to my head. After some time, I awoke, with the sun shining in my eyes. I looked around and saw Sarah bending down over me. I was about to say "Damn you," but only got half the damn out when I felt her lips crushing against mine and felt her wet tears on my face.

She pulled away and laid her face on my chest, exclaiming all the while that she was glad I was still alive.

She lay there, telling me how sorry she was and I, in the meantime, had difficulty trying to understand what had happened.

I was sure of one thing and that was the terrible ache in my head. I almost went unconscious again from the pain. With an effort, I pushed her away and looked at her. I could see the concern in her eyes, so I knew that her tears were genuine.

I told her to go to the stream and get some water. She promptly did as I asked. She put the water on my head and face and the coldness made me think more clearly. I asked her why she had hit me. She said that she did not know it was me. She explained that she had been locked in the cave by someone, but did not know who and thought they were coming back for her. I told her it was Slow Bear and I who had locked her in because she had stolen my money.

She thought about this for a moment, then said to me, "When you brought me here to the Durhams when I was young, I thought when you left I would never see you again. I had followed you when you hid your money, and took it to a safer place. When you returned, I was going to tell you where I had hidden it. But when you threw me in the water, I thought I would let you worry for a while."

I was relieved to realize that she was not a thief, but my anger was not finished. I told her that I could understand the way she felt, but twice now she had hit me on my head and I was afraid that it would not take any more. She had now composed herself, so when I told her this, she laughed, telling me that my head was too hard to hurt much. She went over to the crevice and covered it up as much as possible. She then helped me up the slope and brought the horse over to me. She sat in the saddle and I sat behind her.

When we arrived at the Post, Slow Bear helped me into our room and took care of the horse. I told the

Durhams that I had fallen from the horse and hit my
head. Sarah looked relieved when I said this, but I knew
Slow Bear did not believe me. Mrs. Durham came to
my room and dressed the wound on my head. She was
suspicious of my story after examining the wound, but
said nothing.

Chapter 16
Sarah Grows Up

I was now twenty-two years of age and Slow Bear was close to twenty. Sarah was closing in on fifteen, but acted as if she were older. She did not visit with me while my head healed. I saw her a couple of times with Slow Bear. She was beginning to ride one of the horses. Mrs. Durham had taught her to read and write English, and an Indian woman who did housework around the Trading Post had helped her to understand and speak the Iroquois language.

When she was around the Trading Post, Sarah wore White woman's clothes, but when she went into the countryside she preferred to dress like an Indian male. This gave her more freedom of movement than a robe or dress. She would wear either an Indian leather top or a White man's shirt and either a White man's riding pants or short pants with leggings of leather. Her shoes were always moccasins that were either low or high, depending on the weather. She wore a beaded headband with her hair in two braids which hung each side of her face.

It seemed to me as though she was born to ride a horse. When the animal was running she looked as though she were part of it. Both horses liked her and she them. Mrs. Durham finally put a stop to Sarah's continual riding. She said that she was neglecting her duties around the Post and not doing any school work. Mrs. Durham also was not pleased that Sarah behaved like a tomboy. She was always complaining that Sarah's behavior was not acceptable conduct for a young English lady. I was sure at times she forgot that Sarah was a half-breed like

I was and considered us to be as much her children as Peter. This pleased both Sarah and me.

One evening Slow Bear asked if he could take one of the horses and visit our mother in her village. I agreed and said that I would accompany him. When Sarah heard this, she insisted that she be allowed to go with us. At first Mrs. Durham objected, but Mr. Durham interjected and so she reluctantly agreed. We spent the next few days getting ready for our trip and early one morning we left the Post, promising to return as soon as possible.

It was surprising how much time was saved with horses to ride. Sarah rode behind me part of the day and then behind Slow Bear the remainder. This gave the horses equal treatment, although Sarah was not very heavy. We had many gifts in our saddlebags for our Indian family and that was added weight. We were not in a hurry to get to our mother's village, so the horses had plenty of time to feed and rest.

We passed from Seneca into Cayuga territory without any problems. The people were friendly and helped us with food and a place by their firepits to hear stories and the latest news. We were told that a great ceremony would be taking place in the Onondaga land by the sacred tree and firepit. It was to mark the work and leadership of Chief Metoac, their greatest Chief. I had never met this man, but his fame had spread throughout the Iroquois nation.

It took us ten more days before we arrived at our mother's village. Our coming meant much joy to her and the rest of our relatives. They had heard many stories and tales of Slow Bear and my war on the French. As usual, the stories became more grand and important with each telling. We were credited with many more heroic deeds than we could possibly do in one lifetime. We did not try to correct these stories, for it would seem as if we were trying to appear humble.

My mother took Sarah in hand and saw to it that she was dressed in the clothes of her tribe. She also helped her in getting to know the other women that were her age and still unmarried. Most Indian girls of fifteen were married and had children. Those who were not married by then were not looked down upon, but were given special privileges. Usually it would be a chance to show off their special skills, such as making clothes and jewelry and the cooking, drying, and preparing of food. They were also given prominent seating positions at all ceremonial and tribal gatherings.

Sarah seemed to like the other girls her age and stayed with them every chance she had. I, in the meantime, spent most of my time with my mother and grandfather. Theirs was the central tribe of the district, and most of the important ceremonies were held here. Plans were going on now to honor the great Chief of these people. My grandfather took me to the lodge of Chief Metoac and he made me welcome. We sat for hours it seemed, discussing the English and French and their relationship with our people.

It was apparent why he was such a great Chief. He had a grasp of all the situations and problems to do with his people. His sense of humor was evident when he spoke of the White Man. This was not a man to be fooled. Suddenly, he asked me, "Where does your loyalty belong? You are Indian and you are White—which of these do you try to be?"

The question took me by surprise, but I answered unhesitatingly. "They belong with the people of my mother. I am proud of the traditions of the Indians, as well as their behavior toward one another. The White Man appears to have no loyalty except to greed."

I continued, "They profess to have a great religion, but do not practise it; they have a justice that applies only to how they perceive it, and not to our people."

Chief Metoac smiled and said, "I have heard what

you have done with the White Man and it makes me happy that you take advantage of them and not your brothers."

"Please understand," I said. "When I am with the White Man, I act as a White man, but when I am with my own people, I act like them. When I am with the White Man I am bad, but with the Indian, I am good."

He laughed at this, knowing I had been to the English country and gone to school there to learn how to behave as they do. Then one of the Clan Mothers brought us food and drink. Later, Grandfather and I took our leave. My grandfather was happy because he realized that I had made a good impression on the Chief. I hoped that this was so, because in later years I knew I might possibly need his friendship.

The next morning, I noticed that Sarah was not in the lodge. My mother informed me that she was with the other girls, making things for the coming ceremony. I had not seen her for a couple of days, so I thought I would find out how she was coping with the strangeness of living in an Indian village. Following my mother's direction, I came upon the girls, sitting in a circle, making things with cedar bows.

Suddenly I stopped, as I couldn't believe my eyes. The girls were all naked to the waist. I knew young unmarried girls did this, but not girls of this age. Sarah was just as they were and her pale flesh made her stand out from the other girls. It was plain to see that she had white blood in her. I spoke to her, trying to show no surprise at the way she was dressed—or rather undressed—and asked her to come with me. She accompanied me to a stream. I told her that she should not sit around exposing her breasts to everyone.

She laughed and said it was I who had told her to act like a White person when with them and like an Indian when with the Indians and this is what she was doing. I realized that what she said was true. I was baffled as to what to say next and tried to save face. I told her that her colouring was different and that her nipples were pink, while Indian girls had dark ones. She laughed again and said that her eyes were blue, while their eyes were black, so what was the problem?

Again I could think of nothing to say and tried to believe that it really didn't matter to me how she dressed. But suddenly, I knew that it did, and that I was jealous of other men looking at her.

I knew I was standing there like a dummy. Sarah suddenly hugged me and kissed me on the cheek, saying she would make a bargain with me. She would keep her top on, if I kept my pants up. She then went back to the other girls, laughing and looking at me over her shoulder.

I looked at her, thinking what a bitch she was and feeling somehow that I had made a fool of myself. I went to the lodge and had Slow Bear saddle the horses and we went for a ride into the forest. He knew that something was bothering me, but didn't say a word. I asked him what he wanted to do now that the fighting with the French was behind us. He said that he had made no plans and was waiting for me to decide what we were to do.

This bothered me, knowing he was relying on me to decide his future and I felt responsibility for him. I looked at him and realized that I really loved this brother of mine and would never do anything to hurt him. By Indian standards I had made him a wealthy man. He, as well as I, had many gold coins and so had no need to work for the rest of his life, if that is what he wanted. But he was so innocent that he did not know how wealthy he really was.

I was now mature, weighing about a hundred and eighty pounds. I stood about five feet eight inches tall. My shoulders were wide and my hips narrow, with not an ounce of fat on me. My hair was black, but my eyes were, as they had said, ice blue. I had the features of an Indian—high cheek bones, deep-set eyes, but I had a light-coloured skin. Slow Bear was built very much like me, but had dark skin with black eyes. He weighed about ten pounds less than I, and walked with that peculiar Indian gait, rolling with every step, and moving quickly. He was considered very good looking and had many Indian girlfriends, but had been able to avoid getting married.

The day of the ceremony arrived and so did hundreds of people from other tribes and areas to help celebrate. Chief Metoac was thought highly of and all wanted to show their respect. My grandfather had a part in the ceremonies, so his family members were given preferred seating during it.

The visiting Chiefs and Shaman wore their best finery. The feathers and beadwork were beautiful to see. Their women had worked many long and hard hours on them. The women of our tribe had made decorations that hung from the lodges and longhouses. Wildflowers decorated the poles that were placed throughout the village.

The first night of celebration was taken up with speakers from other tribes paying tribute to the Chief. Many gifts were given. After this, there was food and drink provided for everyone. All this had been prepared days in advance by the women. For the next two days there were celebrations and dancing, nonstop. On the third day, the guests began to leave and within two days, everything was back to normal.

This was a sign that Slow Bear, Sarah, and I should make our way back to the Trading Post and the Durhams. We still had not made plans for our future. I had made many good contacts with other Chiefs during the celebrations and they seemed to like me. Perhaps this would be an advantage to me in the future. It was, before I realized it.

Chapter 17
A New Proposition

When we approached the Trading Post some time later, we noticed strange horses in front. Horses were still uncommon in our area, so it was unusual to see them. As we got closer to the Post, a figure emerged, took the reins of the two horses, and led them to our barn. I suddenly recognized Peter, son of the Durhams.

I gave a shout and Peter turned to see us approaching. I put the horse into a gallop, forgetting that Sarah was sitting on the horse, not the saddle. She gave a curse and grabbed the reins, stopping the horse. I told her I was sorry, but she jumped to the ground, telling me what a stupid person I was, and walked away, rubbing her bottom. Slow Bear and Peter laughed at me and I found myself getting angry. I dismounted and greeted Peter warmly, and we stood talking for a few minutes. Peter told me he was accompanied by Mr. Butler, who wanted to see me.

I had not bothered to call at the Trading Posts. The traders were having enough trouble with the French. Mr. Butler had written to me, saying that I should sit tight for a while, so I was surprised that he had come to the Post. Peter, Slow Bear, and I tended the horses and then went to the Post building.

Mr. Butler and the Durhams were sitting at the kitchen table when we entered. Mr. Butler greeted me as though I were a long-lost son. Sarah was nowhere to be seen. Mrs. Durham made a lunch and we gossiped for a while over hot tea.

Mr. Butler finally told me that he was here on business and had a job for me. He had been contacted by the

British government to line up an interpreter who could work with the Native People. He would be required to work with a British official who was due to arrive in the New World in a month or so. He was to introduce this official to the Indian leaders and help negotiate and make land deals for colonists, who were now coming to the New World in droves.

It would be necessary for me to work closely with this official who was the representative of the Crown. I was told that he was a middle-aged gentleman of high rank and had been a Major in His Majesty's armed forces, though now retired. He had recently married a highborn lady, who was rumored to be many years younger than he. I would have to live in the White Man's village near the salt water which I now knew was called the Atlantic Ocean.

This job was to pay me well and I could have an assistant, which they preferred to be an Indian. I looked at Slow Bear and he was grinning with anticipation that I would accept this position. I told Mr. Butler that I would think about it and let him know before he left. He told me he was leaving the next morning, so the pressure was on me.

That night, Slow Bear and I discussed the offer and he was willing to go with me. Sarah joined us and said she hoped we would not go. She never mentioned her show of temper with me that afternoon, nor did I. After they retired, I sat up late wondering what I should do. I had thought that I would be offered a Trading Post to manage, but Mr. Butler said that I would be more useful to the Trading Company if I accepted the new position.

The next morning, I told Mr. Butler that I would accept his offer. This made him very happy, so we set about making plans. We had over a month before I was to start work for the representative. It was important that all plans were made beforehand. Mr. Butler said it would not be necessary at the onset to take my horses. Most people in town used a horse-drawn carriage and I would find this more convenient for the time I was to be there. It was also difficult to find a stable for horses within the village. I could, however, have the horses brought down when I required them by the Trading Post wagons that brought trade goods to the village.

We discussed many things that day. One of the most important issues to me was what was going to happen to the Trading Posts that were now proving to be unprofitable for the company. He told me that the company was expanding to the west, where there were more animals available and where there seemed to be a never-ending supply of furs. The Posts around us were now being closed. In some cases, traders who had been with the company for many years were given the property that the Posts occupied.

Most of the older Post managers did not want to move further west. Mr. Butler said that the Post the Durhams ran would be offered to them, if they wanted it, but they had already indicated that they wanted to join their son Peter in the big village. I asked him if the Post could be included in the deal with me. In other words, I could have the Post, if the Durhams did not want to keep it. He assured me that it could be included and he would have papers made out to that effect when he was in the White Man's village.

That afternoon Sarah and I went for a ride on the horses. Later, by the stream, I told her what plans had been made. I asked her if she would care for the horses during my absence and she said she would. I could tell something was bothering her and asked what it was. After a long silence, she said she was worrying about her future.

She was concerned, being a half-breed as I was, where she belonged. She knew she could not be Indian and live as they do, but then again, she could not be White either. As long as the Durhams had the Trading Post she would be able to live with them. Lately they had been talking about retiring and moving to the White Man's big village to live near Peter.

I then told her of the deal I had made with Mr. Butler regarding taking over the Post. I said she could live there as long as she wanted. With my leaving she was anxious about her future. She knew she could live in my mother's village, but this is not what she wanted. I told her that she would never have to worry, because I loved her and would take care of her.

She looked surprised, then said she did not want me to be her father. Not giving me a chance to answer, she jumped up, mounted the horse and rode away, leaving me sitting there looking after her. I suddenly realized that what I had said was not intended to make me her father, but that I genuinely loved her and wanted to make her my woman.

I sat there for quite a while, thinking about this, but was no further ahead with plans. I knew that with my leaving within a month, there was no time to actually court her. How could I make her understand my feelings without making a damn fool of myself again?

I returned to the Post and could see that Sarah had stabled her horse. I went into the kitchen. Mr. Butler and the Durhams were drinking tea. Sarah was sitting with them. She did not drink tea, as she hated the taste. She was laughing and talking with Mr. Butler and I could tell he was quite taken with her. She gave me a look and there was something in it that I could not understand.

There was a question in that look, as though she felt abandoned and I was her last hope. The Durhams knew something was wrong, but never questioned us. They thought Sarah was angry because I was leaving again. Mr. Butler and Peter left later that day with the promise that they would send a carriage for me on a certain day. The trip to the White Man's big village would take a long time, even with the carriage.

Chapter 18
How the Indians Were Coping

It is difficult to describe the changes that had taken place since my father, Running Bear, had died. The White Man was now coming into the New World in increasing numbers. At the beginning of the influx, there were the explorers, then the fur traders, and now the colonists, who took the land from the Indians for farming. They had no idea of the effect this had on the Natives.

Our culture was constantly under attack. The White people made no attempt to let us preserve our culture, but instead made every effort to have us accept theirs. Our religious beliefs and way of life were made out to be wicked. Their goal in life, it seemed, was to save us from something that we had lived with in ignorance for so many centuries. More centuries than they had lived in their own.

Our religious beliefs had been with us for thousands of years, whereas their beliefs had been with them only a few hundred years—except, in one case, some six thousand years. We were comfortable with what we believed. It suited our purpose and culture. But because it was so different from the White Man's concepts, it was declared wrong and we were told we were heathens. I can only say that the Indians had no thieves, no prostitutes, no policemen, no illegitimate children. Nor did we have poor people who were put in confinement because they could not pay their debts. In fact, we had no jails.

I might also add that to us, we had no sins. Sins were not defined in our religion, so did not exist. This meant that we did not have to pay someone so that we could have forgiveness for that which we did not commit. That is not to say we did no wrong. What we did wrong was usually against nature and not mankind. If it did happen—say a man killed another of his tribe—he was made to carry the dead body tied to his back for three days. After that, he had to support the family of the man he had killed for the rest of his life.

If an Indian did not obey the rules of the tribe, he was in danger of being sent into exile. This meant he would lose his identity, family, and friends. As the Indian was a community person, this was a sentence worse than death. He then had no one to rely on for help. He had no possessions or rights. Other Indians and tribes would have nothing to do with him. He would be a nobody, a restless soul with no future or any kind of life.

The Native shared what he possessed because every person was considered to be part of his family, even strangers. In most ways, animals were considered to be relatives to man and therefore part of his family. He was born with an obligation to protect all living things, since his own life depended on them. He killed only for food. Unfortunately, most Indians were now becoming inflicted with a disease called greed. The Indian got it from the White Man, who gave him things that he had never seen before for the traded animal skins.

The White Man had now become almost as numerous as the Indian. They had first settled along the shore of the great salt water, which was to the south of our territories. Now they were moving into our areas in alarming numbers. Complaints had been made to the English Crown. The man who was appointed to help in the fair transition of land would be the man that I was to work with.

Over time, Indian trails had become pathways, since they were being used by horses. Now they were used by the White Man's wagons and had become wider paths and even roads. Thus carriages were being used to transport people between populated areas. Many Indians had horses and also cattle, which the White Man had brought with him. These were new to the Indian. These animals had been acquired through land trade.

The dreaded White Man's diseases were still breaking out in many places, affecting both White Man and Indian. One village of White people was wiped out with smallpox. Many Indian villages suffered the same fate. Venereal disease was quite common.

The White Man had explorers who were going further to the west and discovering new lands. Fur traders followed and set up Trading Posts. They had discovered the great salt water in the far West. Many White people were surprised to learn that most Indians had known of this land to the west and of the salt water, long before the White Man had come to our country.

We too had explorers, but we did not call them that. We referred to them as storytellers. They would entertain the tribes they visited with stories of these distant lands and their people. We had some buffalo skins that had been traded through to us from the flat lands of grass. I had also seen skins of a giant lizard from the far south, where they lived in abundance in a huge marsh.

I had seen green carved stone and blue stone jewelry from the south and beautiful feathers from birds that did not live in our area. There were tools and jewelry made of copper, coloured beads of many different stones, and a white metal called silver, that had been traded from the south up to our area.

We were not as isolated from each other as the White Man believed we were. We gathered many ideas from other people and they from us. Our laws and religion were the result of thousands of years of experience, living in our environment. True, there had been many times when people went hungry because nature did not provide what was needed. But we had learned to dry and store meat, berries, fish, and vegetables during abundant times for use when these foods were not plentiful.

We had Medicine Men who took care of our health problems long before the White Man came to our shores. The Shaman knew of many ways to heal us by using various herbs and plants. We used sweat lodges for cleansing and healing. Some of the White people looked upon these practises with scepticism. A few called them witchcraft. Not all White people felt this way, as there were those who visited the Shaman and Medicine Women to learn the benefits of these herbs, plants, roots, nuts, and bark of certain trees. Many of the White people owed their lives to the Shaman who cured them when they had no one else to turn to.

The food crops the Indians grew kept many settlers from starvation. Tobacco is one crop the Indians introduced to the White people. Some say it has been their revenge upon them.

The White Man could not have explored land to the west if he had not had the Indians to help him. They showed them the way. In a peaceful manner they had been introduced to Indian tribes on their westward journey. No doubt you have seen pictures of Indians with a blanket draped over one shoulder, the reason being to leave one arm free to enable them to gesticulate, or make signs, to help them converse with the White people.

Despite the Indians' willingness to share with the White Man, they have been dispossessed from their lands. They have been separated from their source of food, clothing, and medicine. Their culture has been all but destroyed.

Chapter 19
My New Position

Once again I went to work for the White Man, in their large village by the salt water. I really did not know what to expect of the man I was to work for. His name was Farnsworth and he had been an officer in the Imperial Army, as they called it. It turned out that he was a Major. I addressed him as Major from the time I met him.

The days before I left the Post were spent packing and getting ready to leave. Slow Bear went again to see our mother, but I wanted to spend the time with Sarah. She was very depressed because we were leaving. I left the money in the cave where Sarah had hidden it and told her that if anything happened to me, it was hers.

One day I went to the stream and, removing my clothes, went for my usual swim. Again, I was careless, because suddenly my leg was seized and I was dragged under the water. I kicked myself free and went to the surface for air. Sarah's head broke water beside me and she laughed because I was so surprised. I lunged at her and grabbed her around her middle and pulled her underwater.

It was then I learned she was as naked as I was. I let go of her in my surprise and rose to the surface. She too rose to the surface and grabbed me around the neck and tried to submerge me once again. I broke loose and swam to shore, with her right behind me. I walked up to the shore and sat down. She followed.

I lay down with my back to her and she stepped over me and lay down facing me. Her face was inches from mine and she laughed. "Are you so shy of me that you do not like to see me naked?" she asked. "Years ago you were not so shy."

"Years ago you were not a fully developed young lady," I replied.

"Well, I am now and what are you going to do about it?" she asked.

I could not answer that question, but managed to say, "If you were any other young lady lying naked beside me, I would mate with you, but for some reason, I am afraid."

She lay there, thinking this over for a moment. I said, "Perhaps if you hit me on the head with a rock like in the past and kissed me it would make a difference."

She laughed and then went quiet, looking into my eyes. She then kissed me a long, lingering kiss. I pulled her close, feeling her firm body pressed to mine. But something was different. I was not as aware of her body as I was the person within it. Before, when I was with a woman, I was only concerned about her body and the use I was to put it to. This time I was only conscious of the person within the body.

Suddenly she pulled back and looked at me. I said to her, "You must have found a stone somewhere, because I feel like I have been hit with something."

She replied, "It must have hit us both, because I feel the same way."

We lay there talking for the next two hours, and finally, with darkness approaching, we dressed and returned to the Post. The Durhams looked at us and wondered where we had been. They had eaten the evening meal without us. I told them that Sarah and I were to become man and woman as soon as we could arrange the necessary ceremony. They were very happy for us.

Plans were made at a nearby Indian village for us to be made man and woman. This ceremony was almost the same as those in all tribes of the Iroquois, with little changes made to accommodate the local tribal history.

The Shaman

This tribe, called the Wenro, was not actually part of the Iroquois Confederation, but were closely related to the Seneca. There were no boundaries marking each territory because they were considered to be one people. Each tribe held a different ceremony and did what suited them best. I will describe the ceremony that was performed for Sarah and me.

On the day appointed for our ceremony which would be called a wedding, Sarah and I were dressed in special garments. Both of us wore short leather pants and a leather vest that were decorated with beadwork and feathers. We wore leggings that had fringes at the side and were decorated with beadwork. On our feet were moccasins, also adorned with much beadwork.

Over this, we put on a cover that was really a round leather circle with a hole cut in the centre where our head came through. It hung down to just below our armpits. It was highly decorated with beads and paintings. These two covers were the property of the tribe and were used only for this purpose. The Chief wore similar clothing, except his headdress was spectacular. It was made with many coloured feathers and animal fur and hung to the ground. This particular headdress was used only on special occasions. Each feather and fur had a special meaning.

The Shaman was dressed in the most outlandish costume. It was similar to ours, but more elaborately decorated. On the front of the vest, alongside the beads and feathers, there were human and animal bones, hanging loosely. His headdress was a wolf's head—not a copy, but the real thing. The skin had been taken from the head of a wolf and then made to look as though the animal were alive.

Over his shoulders the Shaman wore a cloak like none other I had ever seen. It was covered with the breasts of the male wood duck, with the feathers intact. The cloak was a thing of much beauty. In his hands, he carried rattles and other charms that were made of bones, feathers, and sticks.

Another person who had an interest in the ceremony was the Tribal Historian. This person kept what they called a wampum belt. It was a beaded strip of leather. The beads told the history of the tribe and its people and could be read only by the Keeper of the Belt.

This strip of leather he wore around his waist. His upper body was covered with a breastplate of leather, decorated with many designs and colours. He wore a breechclout and moccasins. On his head there was a goose—not a live goose, but one that had been gutted and dried, to fit over his head. This head of the goose was made to look natural, too.

After many hours of talk by the Chief and Shaman and after we were decorated with flowers, feathers, and animal furs, we both stepped into the Circle of Life. It was made with many different-coloured stones formed into a circle. Each stone represented a historical event in the village tribe. While Sarah and I stood within the circle, still wearing our regalia, each stone was "read" by the Shaman.

Near the end of the ceremony, the Shaman removed his cloak and placed it over both Sarah and me. This was to show that we had entered the Circle of Life as two people, but now we were one. After the ceremony there was food and drink for everyone, which I provided. Then we all danced until the light appeared in the eastern sky.

Sarah and I went to a lodge that had been prepared for us and there we consummated our marriage. I found Sarah to be a virgin. I was surprised that at her age and in our society she could still be. She confided in me that she had not known what race she would end up with—Indian or White, but now she had both in me.

The next day we returned to the Post with the Durhams. They had been with us during our marriage ceremony.

Mrs. Durham let us know that we would not be properly married until we had a ceremony with a White English minister. Perhaps some day in the future we knew we might oblige her, but now we had more pressing matters to attend to.

I was to leave in two weeks' time and arrangements must be made for Sarah. The Durhams insisted that she stay with them during my absence. When I was established, I was to send for her. This pleased neither Sarah nor me. We realized, however, that it was the best plan available to us at the present time.

Slow Bear came back and was pleased that Sarah and I were now man and woman. He was happy to have her as a sister-in-law. This was important, for, according to Indian custom, if anything happened to me he was to take care of her. She would be as a second woman to him. I sent word to my mother that Sarah and I were now man and woman, but by the time she replied, I was gone.

Chapter 20
The White Man's Village

The day of our departure came all too soon. Sarah and I had talked for many hours and we were prepared for our separation. She would be in good hands with the Durhams. The carriage arrived as scheduled. With sorrow we loaded our belongings and took our leave.

For the first few hours, Slow Bear and I were quiet. We were brought out of our thoughts when we had to help the driver overcome some obstacles on the trail. He found it difficult to manage the horse and carriage over the rough trail. At times we would come to a tree that had fallen across the trail, or have to contend with a fast-running stream. Usually the problem was deep mud, the result of a heavy rainfall. Regardless of the cause, the going was slow and tedious.

We slept in the forest at night, bedding down under the carriage. By frequently tethering the horse near grazing land we enabled it to rest. The carriage driver was an Englishman named Hunter. He had been to the Post many times to take in trade goods and bring out furs. Hunter was friendly and knew his job well.

When the opportunity presented itself we stayed at an Indian village or a White settlement, making our meals and sleeping arrangements easier. There were so many White people's villages now that most of our nights were spent in one of them. The further south we traveled, the more civilization we encountered. Not much interest was shown toward us, for it was common now to see Indians and half-breeds together. We passed through several Dutch settlements. There was a scattering of German settlements along the way, too. It seemed to me that people from other countries were now moving to this land.

Because the carriage could travel on better-established trails, I spent the time dozing whenever I could. We offered a ride to people who were traveling in the same direction. Hunter told us this was the expected thing to do.

Finally, after four weeks of travel, we arrived at the White Man's largest village. How it had grown! I had seen it for the first time when I was on my way to England. No longer were there barricades surrounding the village. British soldiers were everywhere. Merchants lined the streets with various things for sale. Slow Bear was enthralled with all the activity.

Hunter took us to an inn that was close to the waterfront and docks. We were given a room on the second floor, facing the water. From the window we could see the great ships loading and unloading cargo. This truly was an experience for Slow Bear. He sat by the window for hours at a time, looking out at the scene below.

We had a meal in the inn that evening, then retired early. Slow Bear could not get used to the bed, so he took a blanket and curled up on the floor to sleep. When I awoke at daybreak he was already seated at the window, chewing on some dried venison. He offered some to me and I accepted.

At nine o'clock a carriage picked us up at the inn, then delivered us to the Trading Post warehouse. Mr. Butler, an Army officer, and two other gentlemen were waiting for us. After he had introduced us to his associates, Mr. Butler took us to a table and we sat down. A servant brought us tea and small cakes.

We were told that Major Farnsworth and his lady had arrived the previous day. We were to meet them later for the evening meal. They went over all the plans with great care so I would know what I was dealing with. My job was to keep the Major informed about whatever the Indians wanted in our negotiations with them. The Major and his lady were to take up residence in a village close to the Indian tribe we would be dealing with. He would be accompanied by a few Army personnel, who would protect him if it became necessary.

I told them that the fewer Army people involved, the better, because the Indians were not comfortable with their presence. They were peaceful people and would treat the representative of the foreign monarch with respect. Mr. Butler concurred with what I said, so the two gentlemen agreed to take his word for it.

That evening Slow Bear and I dressed in our best finery, and left the inn with Mr. and Mrs. Butler for the Farnsworths' residence. As we approached the building I could see that it was a log house with a long, open verandah across the front. This made the place look bigger than it actually was.

The Major and his wife were waiting for us. He was a striking-looking man with gray hair and a beard that covered most of his face. He was tall and slender and his eyes were blue and friendly. Mrs. Farnsworth was young. She had fair hair and skin and was full-figured. I could see that she was at least twenty years younger than he. In height, she stood about to her husband's shoulder.

The Major was wearing a suit similar to those worn by most businessmen. Mrs. Farnsworth wore a gown that reached the floor. It was covered with lace and coloured bows. She was very shrewd in her appraisal of Slow Bear and me, and her eyes seemed to look right through us. I could not understand why she had come to this country, knowing the hardships she would have to put up with.

The house consisted of three rooms: a big living-dining area, a kitchen, and one bedroom. The building was constructed of rough cedar logs that were laid horizontally. I looked around the room. A bearskin rug lay on the pine board floor. A fire burned warmly in a fireplace at one end of the room. A table had been set with a cloth cover on it where pewter knives, forks, and spoons were laid out. There were glass goblets for wine or ale at each place setting. Three candle holders, each holding three candles, were placed along the centre of the table.

We were asked to take seats at the table. Major Farnsworth sat at one end and his lady at the other. Mr. Butler and I sat opposite one another at the Major's end of the table. Mrs. Butler and Slow Bear faced each other next to Mrs. Farnsworth. Suddenly the realization hit me that Slow Bear had never sat at a table like this to eat before! At least, not to my knowledge, except for the odd time with the Durhams. He knew nothing of the manners of the White people, let alone how to eat with a knife and fork from a plate. Indians ate with their hands with few manners.

To the Indian, eating was a chore to get over with as quickly as possible. Food was too hard to find to dally over. I was apprehensive as to what Slow Bear would do. I could do nothing now but hope he would follow my lead, or that of the Butlers. He did so at the beginning of the meal. He watched us take the little square of cloth they called a table napkin and place it on our laps and he did the same. But when the Major tucked his napkin under his chin, Slow Bear became confused. He was about to do the same, but I held his hand without being observed by the others.

The meal was served by young Indian girls who had been well trained for the task. I was to learn that their cook was an old Army cook. He had been sent here especially to work for the Major. The first item brought to the table was an appetizer served on a wooden plate. It consisted of small pieces of smoked fish. I could see the concern on Slow Bear's face. When the Indian servant girl came by, he spoke to her in Mohawk, asking if that was all we were to get to eat. She looked puzzled, but ignored him. I touched his leg in warning.

Things were getting very uncomfortable for me. I was trying to listen to the Major and Mr. Butler, while at the same time checking on Slow Bear. The Indian girls then served us a type of clear soup that had been poured into wooden bowls. I sincerely hoped that Slow Bear would not pick up his soup bowl and drink from it, but he did just that! I wondered what would happen next, but Mr. Butler saved the day . . . he promptly picked up his bowl and drank his soup. The Major, sensing an embarrassing situation, did the same. Quickly, I followed their lead, but refrained from making the smacking noise Slow Bear made when he finished his soup.

The two ladies pretended to ignore the situation. They delicately spooned their soup. The main course was then served. It was an English favorite—roast beef and York-shire pudding with mashed potatoes smothered in gravy, individually on large wooden platters. I could see the questioning look on Slow Bear's face, but he kept quiet. Food was not served in individual servings in the Indian villages. All the food was placed in large pots and we helped ourselves to what we wanted. Slow Bear made short work of his dinner with grunts and much smacking of lips.

The English ate at a very slow pace, tasting every mouthful as though it would be their last. To hurry was the worst of manners. Again, Mr. Butler came to the rescue. He said, "Slow Bear must be very hungry after his long trip." The Major, being a good host, promptly ordered another plateful for Slow Bear. After this course they brought dessert. A fruit bowl filled with apples, pears, and plums was placed on the table. Along with the fruit, a bread pudding was served individual in small bowls. Slow Bear managed to eat the pudding in one mouthful and started on an apple, before the rest of us had picked up our spoons. When they finally served an after-dinner wine which Slow Bear refused, I was relieved. When the meal was over the ladies left us. The men wandered out to the verandah, where we were served hot tea. Slow Bear went out to walk by the water.

Mr. Butler and the Major began to tease me about my concern for Slow Bear's dining habits. They said that not all people conform to White standards and they took no offence at other people's ignorance of their customs and lifestyle. This made me feel better. We went on to make plans for the coming weeks. The Major was anxious to meet the Native people and their Chiefs and to start making arrangements for the land trade. He told us that over fifteen hundred settlers were expected to arrive that year. They would require land for farms.

Chapter 21
We Begin to Work

During the next few days the Major, Mr. Butler, and I met often to work out our plans. We discussed at great length which tribe members would take part in the discussions and what items would be acceptable as trade for land. It was decided that horses, farm animals, and birds would be acceptable. The White men were also willing to trade rifles, which the Indians desired very much. The Army, however, was reluctant to let many rifles get into Indian hands.

It was decided that I would leave before the Major and his lady did. This allowed me time to make suitable living arrangements for them in the area where the talks were to take place. I wanted to make certain that the conditions were not too primitive. As far as was possible, all the meetings were to be held in White men's villages. It was up to me to arrange with the Indians to see that those taking part in the trade talks attended the meetings. The Major would be traveling with his own servants. Among them there was a man who had been with the Major during most of his military life. There was also a young woman servant traveling with Mrs. Farnsworth, who was related to her in some way, though she would not be with her when we went to the tribes.

It seemed best to start in the Mohawk area, which was the closest to us. When we were finished there we would go southward to the other tribal areas. It took nearly a week for plans to be completed. When all was ready, Slow Bear and I set off in the carriage that had been provided for us. There were many White people's villages in the area now, so we were able to follow good roads and stay at comfortable lodgings. During this time Slow Bear learned to enjoy the White man's bed, though he still did not want heavy blankets on him. We traveled north, following a great river that flowed out of the Mohawk lake. We passed through the Munsee Tribal land and on to a village called Albany, named after the tribe living there. Most of this land had already been extensively settled by the White Man.

There were several camps of the Mahicans on our route. We pressed on until we arrived at a village that was situated where the Mohawk and Hudson Rivers joined. It had taken us two weeks to travel this far. Upon our arrival, the Chief agreed to see us. We were taken to his lodge. I explained the reason for our being there. He listened patiently, then said, "I will agree to meet this White Chief." He told us that he would send messengers to have other local Chiefs attend our meeting. We set a date for three weeks hence. Slow Bear and I returned to Albany, the White settlement closest to the Indian village.

Before I left Mr. Butler and the Major, an agreement had been made to have our horses delivered to us. I made arrangements to have Slow Bear return to the White Man's village with the carriage to get the animals. I believed he would pass Mr. Butler and the Major on the road so that Slow Bear could confirm the arrangements we had made for the meeting at the Mohawk village with them.

I did not have any work to do for a few days, so I spent the time getting to know the White people and their history. I learned that many of them were poor and had been allowed out of debtor's prison so they could immigrate to the New World. Many of them just wanted a new life.

I spent some time by the river. I realized there was a good possibility a business could be developed here.

By using the river for the transport of people and goods, the roads which were very rough and hard to travel on could be avoided. There was a man on the bank of the river building a raft, which he called a barge. It was being built for this very purpose. Unfortunately, he was underfinanced for such an ambitious project. I felt an interest in his business venture. After a long discussion, it was agreed that I would finance him in return for a portion of the business. I arranged to have a notary draw up the papers for the partnership.

By now I had amassed a considerable amount of money. Much of it had been sent to me by Mr. Carruthers in England, in addition to the money I had received from the Captain of the sailing ship and what I got from the dishonest traders. Some of these funds I gave to my new partner. I knew he was suspicious of a half-breed with so many gold coins on him but he needed the money badly, so did not ask questions. I had taken fifty-two percent of the business, but agreed that he was entitled to a substantial salary for the period of the time spent in building the barge. Later, I was able to swing considerable business our way through Mr. Butler. We called the business Hudson River Transport. I hired an accountant to keep the books and manage the business.

Getting lumber was a problem. I made calls to a few people in the lumber business who had locations by the river. One man I met had a good wood lot where he was cutting big trees. He told me he wanted to buy additional equipment, but did not have the funds. When I heard this I made him a proposition. I would finance the equipment acquisition and have it delivered by barge to his landing if he would supply the lumber that was needed to finish the barge. I also wanted an understanding from him that, if I so desired, I could purchase up to fifty-one percent of this business for an agreed amount.

It took a couple of days to come to an agreement on this proposition and the amount of money I would invest.

When we reached an agreement, I had the notary and my accountant take care of the details. It had occurred to me that while lumber was being used extensively in this large White Man's town, it made sense to use our Transport Company to take it to that market. This town, by the way, was called New Amsterdam.

I was very satisfied with what I had accomplished in the short time I was in Albany. By the time Mr. Butler and the Major arrived, I had taken good care of my own interests.

I was disappointed to see that the Major had brought Mrs. Farnsworth along, but that was going to be their problem. The environment that she would have to face was not a good one. There were only a few places in this area where she could be comfortable.

We spent the next two days going over the future of our negotiations with the Mohawk group. In the meantime, Slow Bear had returned with the horses. They looked well. He had been able to make good time traveling, having ridden them alternately. I told Slow Bear of my business ventures. While I was conferring with the Major he went out to look them over for himself. He reported that they looked good to him.

Chapter 22
Our First Negotiation

On the appointed day, we left for the Indian village. Mrs. Farnsworth and her servant remained in Albany. The trip was uneventful. Mr. Butler and the Major traveled in the carriage while Slow Bear and I rode our horses.

When we entered the Indian village we were surprised to see so many people. Ten Chiefs from as many tribes had arrived to attend the meeting. They had brought Shamans and Advisors with them, along with their various families. A village of around twelve hundred inhabitants had swelled to over four thousand.

We were shown to a lodge where the Chiefs were assembled and we spent the next hour getting acquainted. Their spokesman asked what we wanted of them. Major Farnsworth, looking very important in his Army uniform with its red jacket, spoke for over thirty minutes. The content of his words were: The English King had received complaints from Indians saying they were being unfairly treated in respect to land claims. He told them he was the representative of the King and was here to see that the Indians were to be treated fairly.

When asked how he intended to do that, he replied that he was authorized to give the Indians fair compensation in trade for sharing their land. He told them that many more people were coming here. These people were farmers and would require land to farm. Since the Indians had more land than they required, he, as the representative of the King, was offering to buy the right to use this unneeded land.

A Chief asked to speak and was given permission. He said, "We, the Indians, have had this land for many, many years and I have seen none that we have not used or had use for. The animals that feed and clothe us need much land to live on. The rivers and lakes supply all of us with fish for food. The forests supply us with wood, bark, nuts, and fruit, which we need. The trees give us what we must have for buildings to live in. We also burn the trees to keep warm in winter. If we trade them to you, what will be left for us?"

"You will still have more than enough land for yourselves to live on as you have done," replied Major Farnsworth. "We will give you things for this land that will make life easier for you in return. Look at these two fine horses that two of your brothers have," he said, as he pointed to my two horses. "Just think how wonderful it will be to have such fine animals. Also, we will give you cattle for milk and meat, along with geese and chickens, so you can raise your own food. Think how proud you will be, when you the Chief, will have a fine horse to ride. Would you rather see Chiefs from other tribes have these horses and you none?"

The Chiefs muttered among themselves for some time. Then the host Chief asked, "How much land do you want and how many horses do you give?"

Major Farnsworth said, "We have many families occupying most of the land south by the salt water. This takes in the territory of the Munsee, Wappinger, and Pocumtuc. Here there are still many Indian villages living in harmony with our people. We do not want your people to leave; we just want to share the land. We would like to have access up to the joining of the Hudson and Mohawk Rivers. For this, we will give each Chief here ten fine horses and three saddles. We will also give each Chief ten blankets and one milk cow."

There was a murmur from the people on hearing this offer. The host Chief stood up and said, "We will give your offer much thought and send you word tomorrow on our decision. We ask that Two Faces and Slow Bear remain here on your behalf to answer questions."

Major Farnsworth agreed. Then, after consulting with us, he and Mr. Butler took their leave. They had stressed they thought their offer was generous and were willing to go no further than another ten horses or a few blankets. That night after we had eaten, the Chiefs requested us to come to their lodge.

When we entered, we could see that they sat in a circle, leaving room for Slow Bear and me to join them. The host Chief asked me if I thought the deal was fair. I could only tell him that I would die without my horse. Slow Bear agreed. I told them that ten horses along with blankets and farm animals represented a lot of money to each of them. However, I said the decision was theirs to make.

They discussed the matter well into the night, then seemed to want to reject it. I suggested they make a counter-offer of what they could agree upon. After more discussion, they said they wanted five more horses each, ten more blankets, and a rifle. Guns had not been mentioned by the Major, so I wondered what his reaction to this would be. I told the Chiefs that I would leave in the morning with their offer and return as soon as possible.

The next morning we saddled our horses and rode until we reached Albany. We wasted no time in telling the Major what the Indians requested. However, I increased the number of horses from five more each, to ten. Slow Bear showed surprise when I said ten, but did nothing to correct me.

The Major showed some reluctance about the rifles, but finally agreed. He asked me to return to the Indian village and give them his answer. He said that he would come the next day with an agreement for them to sign. Even though I was saddle-sore and tired, we left after a hasty meal. We arrived at the village just at dusk. The Chiefs quickly assembled.

They waited until Slow Bear and I seated ourselves before asking me the answer to their offer. I told them that their offer was accepted. I said the Major was so happy with the offer that he made an extra gift to each of them of another five horses. I could see the startled faces of the Chiefs and the surprised look on Slow Bear's face. A slow murmur of approval went through the lodge. The host Chief said that they were most happy with the White Chief's proposition and accepted his gift in friendship.

Slow Bear and I were treated to an excellent meal. Then, being tired, asked where we were to retire. We were taken to a small lodge that was off to one side by itself. After settling we were soon asleep. We slept until after sunrise. We were delighted when four young Indian girls brought us water and food. It was a real honor to be served in this way. The girls were there to be used by us if we so desired, but, being newly wed, I declined. Slow Bear, however, was quick to accept their hospitality. In fact, he stayed inside the lodge with them all day. He did not say if he used the four girls or not. If he did I would have been proud of him.

For myself, I took a walk to the nearby creek to enjoy a pleasant swim and sun bath. I was still feeling sore from the long ride of the day before. As I lay there, an old man came along and sat down beside me. He said nothing for a while. He then asked me if I were an Indian or a White man. I must have shown surprise, but the smile on his face showed me he meant no harm or insult.

I told him I had both bloods in my veins, but my heart was with the Indians. He said he knew this, because I had asked for and received five extra horses for each Chief and could have kept them for myself if I wanted. But I had done the honest thing by giving them to the

Born Many Times

tribes. He asked me about the two investments I had
made recently in Albany. He smiled when I showed surprise that he knew. I surmised that Slow Bear might
have told him, or someone else had mentioned it.

He instantly put that suspicion to rest, by telling me
that who had told him was someone I knew not, nor
ever would. I asked him who he was. He gave me his

name, the name of a very famous Shaman of the Mohawk. The name was Born Many Times and I knew he was known for wondrous things he had accomplished during his lifetime. I felt small and insignificant sitting beside such a man. His eyes penetrated my very being and I was humbled beyond words.

He smiled and said, "I am the living Spirit of all the people in all the tribes that live now and have ever lived. Fear me not, for I love all the children of the Great Spirit. You were born with a heavy burden. Do not make the burden any heavier by your actions against one race or the other. You have remarkable talents; use them for the good of those that do not. Your business adventures will be successful—use them for the good of your brothers. These things I tell you, because I know what has been and what will be."

"You have a question?" he asked.

I replied, "Yes. Will what I am doing now harm the Indians more, or less?"

"What is to be, will be. You can only help and cushion the effects within your power. The White men will have their way now and for many centuries, but the Indians will survive and will someday be rewarded for their patience. The Great Spirit will not desert you or his other children."

I sat and thought about what he had said. When I turned to ask another question he was gone. I looked about, then saw him entering the forest, some distance away. What a mysterious person he was! He had given me enough to ponder on for many days.

Chapter 23
Business Continues

I returned to the village and found Slow Bear sitting outside the lodge that we occupied. He was alone, so I told him of my strange meeting with Born Many Times. He was very interested. He had heard of this great Shaman, but then, what Indian had not heard of him many times over? Slow Bear questioned me at length about our conversation. I told him everything. He said he would have to think about this.

The girls returned with food for our supper. After eating we retired early. We could hear some sort of celebration going on most of the night. When we awoke in the morning food was placed by the door for us. We ate, then walked to the creek to bathe. Later we lay on the bank in the morning sun, talking. We knew the Major and Mr. Butler would not get there until midday.

When they arrived all the people of the village were present to greet them. Everyone was smiling and happy. They managed to complete the business in a short time. There was a celebration to mark the occasion. Speeches were made by various Chiefs, who were all vying to out-talk each other. When we could take our leave without offending, we made our exit. We returned to Albany late that night.

The next morning we met for breakfast. The Major was in a jovial mood. He thanked Slow Bear and me for our work on the deal. He said it would not have taken place had it not been for us. I found myself thinking of the words said to me by Born Many Times. I began to wonder if he had actually been to the village that day.

Mrs. Farnsworth

It was planned that Slow Bear and I would make our way to the southern part of the Oneida territory where it bordered on the lands of the Munsee. There were two streams that intersected here and a village was nearby. This was where we were to meet.

The next morning Slow Bear and I left the Farnsworths and Mr. Butler. We returned to the village of the Mohawk before leaving for Oneida territory. I wanted to enquire there if Born Many Times had been in the village. I spoke to the Chief and Shaman of the local tribe. It settled my mind when I learned that he had indeed spent two days with them during the negotiations, acting as an advisor. This made me feel a lot better, as you can imagine.

The following week was spent traveling to the next meeting place and arranging for accommodation. It would have been much simpler if Mrs. Farnsworth had not been with the group. I found her to be an arrogant, stupid woman, who made it plain that she considered herself to be far superior to everyone else. Her constant demands on people were beginning to irritate them. Most of all, her attitude bothered the Indians.

Slow Bear and I disliked her intensely. She treated Slow Bear as if he were a servant, and did not treat me much better. This was only because of my education and knowledge. I never heard her say a good thing about anyone. She constantly complained about everything. Mr. Farnsworth seemed not to notice how she irritated people. I spoke to Mr. Butler about her. He said there was nothing that could be done without offending Mr. Farnsworth. Hopefully she would tire of the accommodation and return to New Amsterdam.

It was unbelievably difficult to transport the trunks and boxes that this woman had for her clothing. The Major arranged to have a second carriage for this alone. For lodging I managed to get the use of an old Trading Post that was near the place where we were to meet the

Oneida. I secured the services of a few Indian women to clean and prepare the building as well as could be done. When the White people arrived, all Mrs. Farnsworth did was to complain about the accommodation that was provided for her. Slow Bear and I were able to ignore her by spending our time in the Indian Village.

The next morning the Chiefs gathered to greet us. They had been advised of our purpose in being there. They held a ceremony of friendship, during which the Shaman asked the Great Spirit for guidance. The Major made a good impression on our hosts because of his uniform and bearing. He smiled and acted very friendly toward the Chiefs.

I told the Major that the Oneida were aware of the trades that had been made with the Mohawk, so he would not insult them by offering less. He felt however, that the Oneida had less land to offer, so should not receive as much as had been given to the Mohawk. I told him any land he got was worth it, as long as the tribe was happy.

He began the negotiations by offering the same as he had given the Mohawk. The Oneida wanted fewer horses and more rifles. This posed a problem. He was loathe to give rifles, because the Army did not approve of this. The Oneida were adamant, so he finally gave in. He gave each Chief ten rifles, fifteen horses, and a few farm animals. The Oneida were pleased with their bargaining, believing they had done better in their trade than the Mohawk had done.

Chapter 24
Dealing with the Onondaga

We now made plans to meet with the toughest group of all. This was the Onondaga, my mother's tribe. The great Chief Metoac would be a hard man to negotiate with. I was concerned for the tribe, but I was more concerned for the Major, for I did not believe the Onondaga would give land at any price. I spoke to the Major of my concerns. Because of this, he suggested that Slow Bear and I go to the Onondaga first, ahead of the others. This would give me time to try to prepare the Chief for the negotiations. I would send word to him when all was ready. He would stay where he was until he heard from me.

It had been decided we would first attempt negotiations with the Onondaga. When we were through there, we would go on to the Cayuga and Seneca tribes. Later we would go south to the Susquehannas. They had a very large territory. We reasoned that it would be to our advantage to finish our business with their neighbours to the north first.

Slow Bear and I left early the next morning. It took about six days to reach our mother's village. She and our grandfather were pleased to see us. Grandfather arranged a meeting for us with the great Chief of all the area, Chief Metoac, and the sub-Chiefs and Shaman. As it would take four days to arrange the meeting, we set the time to meet on the sixth day. We did not want to appear to be in a hurry, because it would make them suspicious of our intentions.

This interval gave us time to visit with our family and the friends we had made here. Onondaga were a kind and gracious tribe, very handsome and proud. Chief Metoac was well-known throughout the Iroquois territory for his wisdom and love for his people. His village consisted of six longhouses and many smaller lodges. Each of those longhouses was in turn run by a Clan Mother. She controlled everything that went on in that longhouse. She also advised the Chief on many things. Women had power among the Iroquois.

My grandmother was the Clan Mother in the longhouse where my mother lived. It was because of this that my grandfather had such an influence on the great Chief. It was necessary to have the Clan Mothers on your side if you wanted to be a good and respected Chief. Chief Metoac was a wise man and included the Clan Mothers' input in all decisions. This was a very busy place because it was the centre of the religious and political activities of the Iroquois. There was always a ceremony or a visiting Chief to attend to. Slow Bear and I decided we should not hold our negotiations here, but find someplace more suitable.

We found a large Trading Post that was close to the village. We spoke to the manager, who agreed it was a good idea to use the Post for the meeting, as it had a large store area. He had a few Indians remove the trade goods to a storage area. The furs were placed in a nearby shed. This gave us a very large open room for the meeting. There was a small log cabin nearby that could be made into living quarters for the Farnsworths. A place was made in the fur storage shed for Mr. Butler. A group of Indians were hired to build suitable lodges for the Chief and his party as quickly as was possible.

Slow Bear and I had a small lodge to ourselves. It was situated at the rear of the Post. This made it possible for us to come and go without causing a stir. However, before the meeting it was decided that Mr. Butler should have this lodge. Slow Bear and I would take the fur-storage shed. This arrangement had some benefits. The furs made a comfortable bed. Also, it would be more private for Slow Bear and his girlfriends, for he had gathered many.

The day and time was arranged. We sent word to the Farnsworths by Indian runners. About eight days later they arrived and then the complaints from that woman started again. She had the best place in the whole area to stay, but objected anyway. She made it plain she thought the place was good enough for Indians, but it was below her expectations for herself.

Immediately, she had a small platform constructed in the room where the meeting was to take place. It was built about four inches above the rest of the floor. It was planned that she and her husband would stand here when the Chief and his group arrived. This meant the Indians would have to look up to them on the platform. This, to her twisted mind, made it look as though they were superior to the Chief and his people.

That afternoon she asked me to come to the Post because she wanted some advice. She was waiting for me when I entered. She asked me how to address the Chief in the Iroquois language because she wanted to impress him and the Clan Mothers. I was speechless. Why would she want to impress them while at the same time she was having a platform built so as to downgrade them? I thought of what an arrogant mindless bitch she was, so decided to think the matter over carefully. Finally, I told her that she should address the Chief by a word that was sure to impress him. I then gave her the Iroquois word for penis. Then, still in the Iroquois language, I gave her the full sentence that she should say. In English it meant, "I am glad to meet you, you prick."

I spent over two hours with her to be sure she had memorized the words with the proper accents where they were needed. After she had learned it correctly, I left.

I found Slow Bear and told him what I had done. He thought it was hilarious and said that he could hardly

wait for the meeting to take place. The next day I began
to have second thoughts about what I had done, but she
soon dispelled them with her domineering attitude. Neither the Major nor Mr. Butler knew Iroquois, so I felt
safe. I knew my Indian friends would not say anything
to give me away.

The great day finally dawned. Chief Metoac and his
group had arrived the afternoon of the day before, but kept
to themselves with their advisors. I had met with them
and the Clan Mothers to let them know what to expect at
the meeting. I did not, however, mention the greeting that

Major Farnsworth and Chief Metoac

I had given to Mrs. Farnsworth. I did not even tell the Chief. I wanted to see how he would handle it.

The Major, with Mrs. Farnsworth by his side, stood at the end of the hall on the platform. Mr. Butler stood on one side, Slow Bear and I on the other. Slow Bear was wearing his best Indian clothes, while I was dressed as a White man. I wore a white shirt, coat, knee britches above white stockings, and black shoes. My hair was pulled back and tied behind my head.

Chief Metoac entered the hall. He was followed by a man bearing furs as gifts for the White Man. Behind the Chief were sub-Chiefs and Shaman, followed by six Clan Mothers. The Chief noticed the platform. He deliberately walked to approximately six feet from the edge of it. The man bearing the furs stood to one side of him, the Clan Mothers on the other. I could see that the Chief had realized the reason for the platform. By stopping six feet away from it, he forced the White man to step down to his level in order to greet him. A wily one, this Chief.

The Major stepped forward and greeted Chief Metoac in English. I interpreted what the Major had said, even though I knew the Chief could speak good English. The translation was for the Clan Mothers. The Major accepted the gift of furs with thanks, then introduced his wife. Mrs. Farnsworth stepped forward with a smug look on her face and said in Iroquois, "I am pleased to meet you, you prick."

There was a gasp from the Clan Mothers and the others of the Chief's party. They wondered what his reaction would be. With a hint of surprise, but unnoticed by the others, he quickly looked at me. A knowing look came into his eyes. He then replied in Iroquois, "I am pleased to meet you also, you cunt. I can see you are a very arrogant and haughty person. Why would any man take you for his woman?" At this, Mrs. Farnsworth beamed. She believed she had shown everyone here just how clever she was.

Chief Metoac had made his reply in such a friendly manner that his response gave the impression of being very pleased by the White woman's greeting. By this time the Clan Mothers, Slow Bear, and I had tears in our eyes from suppressing the laughter we were holding back. The Major turned to me and said, "This must be a very solemn occasion for your people. They all have tears in their eyes. Very touching indeed."

This was too much for my bladder to bear. I promptly wet my pants. I took the furs the Chief had given to the Major and held them in front of me. I hoped no one would notice my wet crotch. I need not have been so concerned because when the Clan Mothers moved to the table for negotiations, I noticed there were wet puddles where they had been standing.

I took this opportunity to leave the room and change into Indian clothes. Later, the Major mentioned that it was good of me to do so, as it made the Indians feel more secure with us. When I returned to the room, everyone was seated at the table. They all seemed to be talking at once. There was an empty chair at the table between the Chief and the Major. I sat down there. Mrs. Farnsworth was seated between Mr. Butler and Slow Bear.

When all was quiet the Major spoke. I translated what he said so the Clan Mothers would understand. He told them his purpose for being there and the business he hoped would be transacted. He then made an offer that was comparable to those made to the Mohawk and Oneida Nations. The Chief quickly rejected it. Although he was asked to say what he was willing to accept, he refused.

He said, "As Chief of the Onondaga, I consider the territory of my people to be a sacred trust. This land is the centre of the Iroquois Nation. It is here that the Sacred Firepit and the Tree of Life are kept for all the Iroquois. Here, too, is where the government of all the Iroquois people meets to handle the affairs of the Iroquois Nation. I could not trade away one inch of this land."

The Major showed instant dismay at the Chief's words and knew that it was useless to argue. As a good host, he did not mention the matter again at this meeting. The next morning he asked my advice. I reminded him that I had told him it was not going to be an easy task. I told him that if the Chief had made this decision, he would not, under any circumstances, change his mind. I told him to wait until the Chief invited him to meet with them again.

I knew the Chief would not accept the hospitality of anyone unless he was able to reciprocate. That afternoon an invitation was received, asking that we meet with the Chief the next morning at his camp nearby. I told the Major to make no new offers, or to even mention the deal, unless the Chief asked about it. It was a game to be played and the Chief held all the power.

Later, at the evening meal, the Major and Mr. Butler were deep in conversation. Slow Bear had left to do his thing. Mrs. Farnsworth and I were alone at the table. She asked me how it felt being neither Indian nor White Man. I told her I had the best of both worlds and used them to the fullest.

She asked me about Slow Bear. She wondered if he had a woman, to which I replied in the negative. She seemed to me now to be genuinely interested in the Indians, especially the women of the tribe. She asked what their life was like. I told her that for the most part they were satisfied with their life. They held most of the power in the tribe and in its functions.

The women elected the Chiefs, but only those who had proved to be good providers and husbands. How a man conducted himself as far as his family and friends were concerned decided whether or not he would be a desirable Chief. There were Hereditary Chiefs who inherited their positions, but had no actual power in the tribe. It was just an honorable position.

A woman of the tribe looked for a man who would provide her with the necessities of life, rather than one just having handsome features. The man wanted a woman who would give him many children and would be a good mother. It mattered not whether she was beautiful. Sex was not something of importance to be pursued, for it was freely available, whether it was with your own woman or someone else's. Living in a building with a number of people who were mostly related did not give them much privacy.

I told her about life in the longhouse, explaining that a woman who had been made Clan Mother was in charge of that particular longhouse. I also pointed out that a person's ancestry or blood line followed that of the mother. For instance, if the mother was a Mohawk, her children were considered to be Mohawk.

Mrs. Farnsworth said she was surprised to learn that the Indian woman had so much influence in the tribe and on its members. It also surprised her to know that the Medicine Women were more knowledgeable in the ways of their craft than were the Shamans. I had the impression that Mrs. Farnsworth had learned in a short time a great deal about our women. I was gratified to hear her say that our women had a better life than the White women enjoyed.

Chapter 25
Grandfather Dies

The next morning a message arrived for Slow Bear and me from our mother, Yellow Flower. It said that our grandfather had died. We made plans to leave immediately. We were not far from her village, and we expected to be there within a day's ride. Chief Metoac sent my mother messages of sympathy. The Major suggested we take the opportunity to visit with the Durhams. It would give me a chance to see Sarah. He was willing to wait in the area, as it was a pleasant place to relax for a while. We accepted his offer.

We were gone within the hour and rode until we arrived at our mother's village early the next morning. She and her family deeply grieved grandfather's death. He had been a good man and the whole village was saddened. Many people came from nearby villages to pay their respects. They had the funeral ceremony for him that day, after which the village Chief had many nice things to say of him. They buried him in the fetal position, sitting up in his grave, as was our custom.

The next two days were spent with many different ceremonies honoring this well-liked man. I knew from my own experience with my grandfather that he was honorable and honest. I was proud that he was my grandfather. My mother took his death very hard, but not as hard as her two brothers did. They paid a few women of the tribe to be mourners who wailed from dawn to dusk until they got on our nerves.

After staying a respectful length of time, Slow Bear and I departed. We left one morning and headed in the direction of the Seneca land. We traveled without much luggage, hoping to reach the Post within a week. As it turned out, our arrival time was delayed by a couple of days.

When we came near the great waterfall, we followed a trail that was commonly used by most tribes as they traveled back and forth. One morning we heard something on the trail ahead of us making strange noises. This made us curious. We hurried to catch up to whatever it was making these sounds. When we topped a rise we could see two men. Another person was bent over, walking on his hands and feet. One man was leading him with a rope which was tied around his neck as if he were an animal.

I asked Slow Bear to stay back and let me go ahead to see what was going on. I put my horse into a gallop and caught up to the people. I turned and faced them. I asked the men what was the matter with the person who was bent over. They laughed and said he thought he was a dog. I looked at the man and could see that his face had been beaten and there were whip marks on his back.

I asked them why they were treating this poor fellow like this. They told me he had been born without a brain. They had bought him from an Indian of the Potawatomi tribe.

They became angry when I continued to question them. They called me a half-breed bastard and threatened me. I dismounted from my horse. At the same time, Slow Bear drove his horse toward them, making them fall out of his way. Before they could recover we pulled our rifles and pointed them at the two men. They knew they were at our mercy. The poor person on the ground crouched in fear. When I approached him he said, "No hurt, no hurt."

I said to him, "No one will hurt you. We are your friends." I touched him on the shoulder. At this, he drew back in fear. I took the rope from around his neck and patted his shoulder. In anger I turned toward the two men and aimed my rifle at them. I said, "Never have I felt like killing someone as much as I do you two."

Slow Bear looked at me and said, "Please do not kill them, Two Faces. They are below that."

"What were you going to do with this poor creature?" I demanded.

"We were taking him home for our children to play with," one said. "He was badly treated by his other owner, not us."

"What did you pay for him?" I asked.

"Nothing," he said. "The man was glad to be rid of him, as we will be if you want him."

Without even thinking about it, I said we would take him. Slow Bear gave a grunt of surprise, but nodded in agreement. I told them to leave us and not bother this poor man ever again. They grabbed their possessions and took off as fast as their feet could carry them. Slow Bear built a fire and prepared a small meal for us. Our new company just sat and stared at us with frightened eyes.

When the meal was ready I took some to him. He put all of it in his mouth at once. I went back to Slow Bear, who had been watching us. I picked up my food and took it over to our guest. The same thing occurred. Slow Bear had begun to eat his portion, but seeing what had happened to mine, gave his to the man also. His meal disappeared in the same manner.

I looked closely at our new charge. He was a giant of a man, with the biggest head I had ever seen. Even though his face was badly marked, I could see that all his features were bigger than normal. His eyes, nose, and mouth were large and fit into a massive head. His arms were as large as my waist and were very muscular. He had broad shoulders and a waist that was almost as big. He was indeed a giant.

When he eventually stood up, he towered to more than six feet and taller when he did not slouch over. He was dressed only in a worn breechclout and had nothing on his feet. I took a blanket from the bag on the horse and gave it to him to cover his shoulders. He looked at it in confusion. I showed him how to place the blanket around his shoulders. Slow Bear and I discussed what we were to do with him. We decided to take him to the Post.

I went over to him and asked him to stand up. He shook his head and said, "Me dog."

I said to him, "You are not a dog, you are a man like me."

He seemed to be confused. I pointed to Slow Bear and said, "You are friend of him and me. You walk like him and me."

It took us over an hour to get him to understand what we wanted him to do. Finally, he stood up. I looked up at him and felt dwarfed by his size. He could have stepped on me like an insect. The average height of an Indian is approximately five foot four inches. So to us, he was a giant. I wondered how he could allow himself to be treated as he had been. I was to learn over time that even though he had the body of a giant, he had the intelligence of a five-year-old child. To avoid any more confusion, Slow Bear and I led the horses and walked along with the man.

That evening, when Slow Bear gathered wood for the fire, the man helped without being asked. We tripled the normal amount of food when preparing our meal, but it was not enough. This person was still hungry. After we had eaten I asked him his name. He answered Fish Head. This was a strange name, even for an Indian. We were to learn later that he was named Fish Head because that was all his family fed him when he was young. When the Indians catch fish they dry some for winter use. In most tribes the heads were fed to the dogs, but some Indians use them to make a fish stew. It appeared his family had fed him the fish heads.

Chapter 26

Home with a Guest

Our new friend sat by the fire all night with the blanket I had given him draped over his shoulders. In the morning we finished what was left of our food supply. It was fortunate that we would reach the Post that evening. As we started to leave we realized that Fish Head was scared of the horses, so he walked along behind us. We kept the horses to a slow pace so he could keep up.

Shortly after dark we arrived at the Post. Sarah flew into my arms when I dismounted from the horse, and we were so happy to see each other. After we had greeted everyone, we introduced them to Fish Head. We gave them a short explanation of why he was with us. As was usual for her, Mrs. Durham took him under her wing. Even though Fish Head was very shy of her at first, he did what she asked of him.

First of all, she asked Slow Bear to take him to the stream by the horse stable and stay with him to be sure he bathed. She found some clothes for him to wear that had been too big for anyone else. They still proved to be too small for him. When she made us a meal she found Fish Head to be more than just a big eater. After the meal Slow Bear and Fish Head went to our room in the stable. I went with Sarah.

In the morning before we dressed, Sarah told me she was expecting a child. This delighted me. She was as happy as I. I held her close and told her it made no difference to me whether it was a boy or girl. When we finally went to the kitchen, the Durhams were happy that I had been told the good news. Slow Bear and Fish

Head came in. This time Mrs. Durham was prepared for Fish Head's appetite.

She had been up for hours, making a large venison stew and many loaves of bread. The meal was so good that even Slow Bear and I had second helpings. Fish

Fish Head

Head's ill-fitting clothes were a problem that Mrs. Durham would soon correct. Somewhere in the place she found a large wool jacket. It fit him. Next, she took a pair of pants and with Sarah's help made them bigger.

In the meantime, Slow Bear measured Fish Head's feet. He went to the nearby village and had a woman make a pair of moccasins for him. They were not the best moccasins, but they did give his feet protection. They would do until we could get a more substantial pair for him. Moccasins were like leather tubes that made an angle at the foot. They could be worn on either the left or the right foot.

Usually I had three moccasins made at the same time. When one of them wore out it was easy for me to replace it with the third one. To make the moccasin wear longer, I had three layers of leather sewn onto the sole. One type of moccasin reached just past the ankle and was worn in the summer. During winter we wore moccasins that reached to just below the knee. Some moccasins were decorated with beads and coloured porcupine quills. However, the most common were made of soft leather without fur. Some tribes preferred leather with the fur still intact. At times they were worn with the fur on the inside, at other times on the outside.

By evening Fish Head was wearing his new clothes. He looked much better. Mrs. Durham said that on the following day she would make a shirt for him to wear under the jacket. All he needed was a hat. Mr. Durham excused himself and returned with a hat. What a hat! It was what was referred to as a stove-pipe hat. I can only describe it as being a tall round black silk cylinder with a covered top and a brim around the bottom. He placed the hat on Fish Head. Although it did not fit, it did stay on his head. We all laughed when we saw him. Fish Head took this as a compliment and would not give up the hat. Mr. Durham said he could keep it as he had no use for it.

Finally we got around to discussing what we were to do with Fish Head. It was obvious to us that he was mentally retarded. We estimated his age in years to be in the late teens, but mentally his comprehension was that of a three- to five-year-old child. Even though he was big and muscular, it appeared to us that he was harmless.

We questioned him about his family, but he could not remember anyone. We believed that he was a full-blooded Indian. He asked if Slow Bear and I were friends. We told him we were brothers. He looked at us closely, then reached over to Slow Bear and scratched his skin. I realized that he noticed I was light-complexioned, while Slow Bear had darker skin. He thought perhaps Slow Bear had darkened his skin. I told Slow Bear this. He laughed. I explained to Fish Head that we had the same mother, but different fathers. He seemed to understand. It showed us he did have some intelligence.

I mentioned this conversation to the Durhams and Sarah. They agreed that there might be some way to help Fish Head. I asked the Durhams how long they planned to run the Post. They said they would not leave before Sarah had the baby. This made me very happy. I told them I wished they would stay with us forever. Mrs. Durham came over and gave me a hug and a kiss on the cheek. She told me that I was a good son. It was decided that Fish Head would stay with them. Perhaps Mr. Durham could find something useful for him to do.

We stayed at the Post for a few more days before we made plans to leave to continue with our work. The Major and Mr. Butler would be waiting for our return. I told Sarah I would be back within the coming month. I wanted to be sure that she would not be concerned for me. Again, it was a heart-breaking farewell. Fish Head cried when we left. I had made the mistake of telling him to take good care of Sarah. He took this request seriously. I learned later that she could do nothing without him being there to watch over her. She could not even have the privacy of going to the toilet without him.

Chapter 27
Back to Work

It took us eight days to travel back to join the Major and Mr. Butler. I learned that the Major had visited with the Chief several times and had made some progress in their talks. It must be remembered that the Indian had given the White Man only permission to use the land and have access to it. This did not give the him title to the land. To the Indian way of thinking, it was still Indian land. The Major understood this. He was trying to get the permission of the Indians in this context. This was the first time they had asked for the Indians' permission, and was not the way it had usually been done.

The Crown was trying to pacify the Indians. They were hoping to receive agreements that would stop future problems for the immigrants. When I spoke to Chief Metoac I explained this to him. He understood what I was saying. He finally agreed to let the White Man have access to a certain part of their land. It was to be understood that it was to be only the use of the land that was negotiated and not the ownership. It was also stipulated that the area being considered was the only part that was implied in the agreement. The White Man was never to be allowed into the place of the Sacred Firepit or the Tree of Life.

After discussing this with the Major and Mr. Butler, the Chiefs gave their approval. A meeting was scheduled for the signing ceremonies. A few days later this was done to everyone's satisfaction. The next tribe we planned to visit was the Cayuga, whose land bordered the Onondaga. We could see no problem with these people now that three of the tribes had made agreements.

I received a request from the Major to visit him the following day. I did. He asked me to go to New Amsterdam with his lady. She was now weary of the accommodation, and preferred to wait in their place in the town. He wanted me to go with her in their carriage so I could protect her and make sure she arrived safely. He said that Slow Bear could help them in the Cayuga district. They would wait for me to rejoin them there.

I did not relish the idea of being confined in a carriage with Mrs. Farnsworth for the week or so that it would take to get to New Amsterdam, but I could not think of a reasonable excuse to refuse. So the arrangements were made for us to leave within three days. When Slow bear heard of the trip, he teased me no end. So much so, that I told him I would arrange to have him take my place if he said another word. He rolled his eyes back into his head, got down on his knees, and begged me not to do so. We both laughed and I told him to behave himself.

Chapter 28
New Amsterdam

Before we left I noticed Mrs. Farnsworth's luggage had been stored on top of the carriage and on the shelf at the back. Several hat boxes had been placed on each seat inside the carriage, leaving just enough room for us. She rode facing the front of the carriage while I faced the back. I carried just one small bag, which I placed on the roof. The weather was very hot and humid. There were openings above the doors which provided some relief from the heat, and the moving carriage created a slight breeze. However, when the carriage stopped the heat seemed to close in on us.

I removed my jacket and unbuttoned my shirt to help keep cool. Mrs. Farnsworth was wearing a dress that was cut low in the front, as were most of her dresses. She also wore a small jacket. She removed the jacket and her hat. She continually fanned herself with a small decorated fan. About midday the driver stopped by a grove of trees near a stream, so we could have a meal. While the driver prepared the food, I excused myself and walked around a bend in the stream. When out of their sight I removed my clothes and went into the water.

I was enjoying the coolness of the water, when Mrs. Farnsworth came along the shore. She saw me in the stream and sat down on the bank to watch me. She then stood up. Pulling up her dress and petticoats, she removed her stockings and the long bloomers White women wore. She sat on the bank of the stream with her feet and legs in the water. She then lay back and from where I was in the stream, I could see all she possessed. Thankfully, the driver called us to eat. Mrs. Farnsworth made no attempt to get up. She just sat there. I was completely naked. She was aware of this, but did not move.

I realized I had nothing that she had not seen before, so I walked out of the water. She followed my every move with her eyes. I stood in front of her and put on my clothes while she watched. When I turned to leave, she snatched up the clothing she had removed and followed me back to the carriage. We ate quickly and were soon on our way again. After the cool swim and a meal, I felt much better. I dozed off as the carriage moved along a road that was fairly smooth.

Suddenly, I was jolted awake as the carriage lurched from side to side. There was just time enough for me to stop the hat boxes from falling on us. The driver stopped the carriage. He came to the door to tell us the road ahead was very bad, that we would be in for a rough ride and we could expect the road to be this way for the next two hours at least. We told him we would hold onto the side straps and watch out for ourselves.

After we had gone on for a few miles, it was obvious that Mrs. Farnsworth was having difficulty staying on her seat. I took the hat boxes from beside her and put them on the seat where I had been sitting. I sat beside her.

In this position I could put my arm around her to prevent her from bouncing around and perhaps hurting herself. I put my feet up to hold the hat boxes and she did the same. Later, I noticed that her dress had crept up to almost her thighs, but she did not seem to pay attention to it. I then noticed that because of the shifting and bouncing of the carriage, the top of her dress had dropped off her right shoulder. Her breast then came out from under the dress. She did nothing about this either, but I was sure she knew.

I tried not to look, but after a while I suppose the male instinct in me became too powerful. I cupped her breast in my hand and began to stroke it. I looked at her. She had put her head back and had her lower lip between her teeth. Without any objection from her, I pulled the other breast from her dress and began to caress it also. I kissed her neck and face. Suddenly, she pulled me close and her lips found mine. Before long we mated in that bouncing, jolting carriage. You have no idea how difficult it was for me to do what was necessary. She wore many petticoats and her dress was heavy and cumbersome. To add to the confusion there were hat boxes and hats everywhere in the way. When it was over we were surrounded by them and I had great difficulty in pulling up my pants.

We spent the next half hour putting the hats into their proper boxes. By the time we were through the road had smoothed out. Mrs. Farnsworth had pulled herself together and was looking out the window at the countryside. Neither of us spoke. The balance of the afternoon was without conversation until we reached the inn where we were to stay the night. It was a small inn and we were given adjoining rooms.

We met later that evening at the dining table. There was still little conversation between us. She had bathed and changed clothes, so looked refreshed. I had gone to a nearby stream to bathe. After the meal she excused herself and went to her room. I went outside to the verandah. I spent the next two hours drinking tea and talking with the inn owner and our carriage driver. Finally, I went to my room and to bed.

Within the hour I felt someone get into the bed beside me, throwing her leg over and straddling me. It was Mrs. Farnsworth. She proceeded to seduce me and I was not unwilling. Later we lay exhausted. It was then she began to talk. She told me she was not really a bad woman, but because she was married to an older man, she could not have sex when she desired it. This made her very frustrated. When she saw me naked, she had made up her mind that she would have me.

She told me she had learned from Mrs. Butler that in England I had a house of ill repute. Also, that I was not above making love when I could. This might have been true, but because I was Indian, it was the way I had been raised. She asked me if all Indians were as well endowed as I was. I told her it was probably because I was of mixed blood. I told her also that we Indians had a saying, "Use it or lose it." Again I used it, for the third time.

About an hour later she left to go to her own room and to bed. By now I was tired out and fell fast asleep. The next morning I again went to the stream and bathed. By the time I returned to the inn, a meal had been prepared. Soon we were on the trail again. It was a warm day, but not as humid as the day before. We passed through many small White Man's villages. Around midday we stopped at one for lunch.

Mrs. Farnsworth never mentioned our activities of the previous day. She spent most of her time dozing or looking out at the passing landscape. For my part, I was happy to be able to rest and think this thing through. I felt no remorse for my infidelity. What had happened was the custom among my Indian people. But for the White Man, it was a very different matter. Even though it was frowned upon if a man had sex with a White woman who was not his wife, they would take advantage of a chance to have sex with an Indian woman. It was therefore well within my conscience to believe that I was taking revenge on the Whites by using one of their women.

At dusk we stopped at an inn for the night. Mrs. Farnsworth sat next to me at the table during the evening meal. The driver and another man sat opposite us. Whenever I could without the two men noticing, I would run my hand up along the inside of her leg. She pushed my hand away. I persisted. Finally she excused herself and went to her room. She did not return to the living area that evening.

After talking with the two men for quite some time, I went to my own room. After lying in bed for about an hour, I got up and went to her room. I did this without being observed. She was in bed asleep. There was a candle on the table by the bed. She had gone to sleep without extinguishing it. I sat at the edge of the bed looking at her. She was wearing a nightgown, but the neckline was low-cut. It was not hard to lower the gown enough to expose her breasts. I began to caress them. She awoke and began to fight me.

I grabbed her hands. While holding them above her head, I lay on top of her. She made no sound, but continued to struggle. I put my head down and caressed her breast with my face and mouth. She became quiet and then quickly became a participant. Never had I been with a woman with such passion. For the next three hours I was "sexually abused," for want of a better description. But, I have to admit I enjoyed it.

When it was over, I lay there with my back scratched and bleeding. My shoulders and neck had bite marks on them. I looked at her. She was still breathing hard and was covered with sweat from the exertion. I left her lying there and returned to my own room. I pulled on a pair of pants and went to a stream nearby. I soaked there for an hour. When I returned to the room I looked at my wounds. Most of them would be covered by my clothing. However, there was a bite mark on my cheek and several on my neck that would be hard to obscure. Fortunately no one mentioned them.

When we met for the morning meal, Mrs. Farnsworth looked as though she had been in a battle. I knew I had. She was in a good mood nonetheless and talked as though nothing had happened. When she got up from the table, I noticed that she moved slowly. I realized she had not come out of our tryst unscathed. I had to help her when getting into the carriage. Later, when we were moving along, she complained that I had been very rough with her. I told her that I, too, had wounds from our activities.

After two weeks we arrived at New Amsterdam. The driver dropped Mrs. Farnsworth off first. He took me to the inn where Slow Bear and I had stayed the last time we were there. The following morning I had a light meal before going down to the docks. There I found an ironmonger. I put in an order for the equipment my partner in the lumber business had asked for: spikes that had loops on the side where chains were fed through; collars with a sharp spike on the end and a sleeve where they could attach a pole, used to push logs in the water; several metal log-turning devices that were attached to a pole; and several yards of one-inch chain to hold the log booms together.

This was going to be a heavy load. I had then to find a person with a good wagon and team of horses to deliver it to the lumber camp near Albany. When I finished my business I began looking around. Here, the Hudson River flowed into the ocean. The White Man had taken up most of the shoreline for docking. However, I found a place that was set apart from the business section of the shoreline. There was a gradual slope down to the water's edge. I located the owner of the property. With hard bargaining, I managed to acquire fifty acres of land, which had about four hundred feet of water frontage. This took every available cent I had with me.

I was on my way back to the inn when I heard someone hail me. I turned in surprise to see the Captain of the boat on which I had returned from England. His name was Captain Stead. He invited me into a drinking establishment close by. He seemed glad to see me. We each ordered a pint of ale.

Chapter 29
A New Business

The first thing the Captain did was give me a small bag of coins. He said the money was from the last trip he had made. He then asked if I was interested in a business arrangement he had stumbled upon. I listened with interest when he told me he could get his hands on a sailing ship similar to the one he sailed as Ship's Master for the Trading Company. The business would take a considerable amount of money, but could put us in the shipping business. This particular ship had been taken from a pirate who had been hanged and his crew imprisoned.

The government of the White people were asking for bids on the ship. Since he was a Ship's Master with many years of experience and contacts, he was sure he could get the ship, but he lacked the finances. He mentioned a sum he thought the ship would sell for. It was a handsome sum, but not one that was out of my reach. I told him I was interested, but wanted to think it over carefully as it was a major investment. He assured me I could take all the time I required. He said that it was fortuitous indeed that we had met. I told him where I was staying and to contact me there the following evening.

I went back to the inn where I was staying. I had a late meal before retiring. Earlier, the owner of the inn had cautioned me about wandering around the docks after dark or going to the several bars that served the area. It appeared that men who were alone or who had too much to drink were easy prey for some ship Captains to add to their crews. They referred to this as being "shanghaied." Many of these men were never heard of again. Naturally it was illegal, but who was there to inform? As it was a tough neighbourhood, one would be foolish to be about after dark.

Early the next morning I went to see a lawyer-accountant who had been recommended to me by the innkeeper. He was a young man in his middle thirties. When I mentioned the "boat bidding" to him he told me he was aware of it. He suggested a price much lower than Captain Stead had mentioned, saying the only other bidder would probably be the Trading Company. I told him of my other business endeavors. He agreed they would be undoubtedly profitable. I hired him as my lawyer, accountant, and business advisor. I had him close the deal I had made on the shoreline property.

Later, when the Captain arrived at the inn, we went to the dining room for a midday meal. I told him I was interested in bidding on the boat, but wanted to see what repairs were needed to make it seaworthy again. He agreed it would be a good thing to do. After our meal we went to the dock where the ship was moored.

It was a big ship. It had three masts and rode high in the water. We were given permission to board. I was surprised to see the armament that were still on board. Cannon were lined up on both port and starboard sides. Some damage had been done to the rigging when the ship was taken from the pirates. There were bloodstains on the deck. Below was empty of anything that was useful. There were barrels and boxes strewn about. The crew's quarters were in a terrible state. Empty bottles and casks were everywhere. Stale urine made a terrible stench.

The Captain's quarters was not in much better a state. Clothes and papers were everywhere. We saw many articles of women's clothing. The Captain laughed and said, "They did take some prisoners." Out on the rigging the Jolly Roger hung in tatters. The Union Jack hung above it on another mast. I told the Captain to have the ship checked by a good millwright. He agreed to do this. I told him that my lawyer was drawing up a bid to present to the government.

We returned to the inn in time for our evening meal. I told Captain Stead that I would be leaving in the morning because the Major's carriage was returning. When he had gone I took a carriage to see Mrs. Farnsworth to tell her I was going. I was met at the door by her woman servant, who led me into the living room.

When Mrs. Farnsworth entered the room she looked happy and contented. I told her why I was leaving. She asked me pointedly if I were the type of man who had sport with a woman, then bragged about it. I assured her that what had happened between us would stay that way, "just between us." I told her that our encounters were merely sexual and were not intended to express any feelings for each other. I also said that it had been most enjoyable and I would never forget her. She told me it was for her too. Upon leaving she kissed me and wished me well.

I never saw Mrs. Farnsworth again, although I met the Major several times. I heard rumors that she was seeing men behind her husband's back. I was glad I did not have to have anything to do with her. If an Indian, or even a mixed-race man, was caught with a White woman he would be shot or hung. Most of the mixed-breed children were the result of unions between White men and Indian women. Not many White women had mixed-breed children. If a White woman and an Indian man wanted to live together she would be unable to live with the White people. She had to live in the village of the Indian.

Very few White women were raped by Indians, but it was not so the other way around. That is why the majority of mixed-breed children were born to Indian women.

Chapter 30
With the Major Again

Before daylight the next morning the carriage was at the door for me. I sat up front with the driver because I wanted to speak to him and ask him for some advice. I wondered if he knew anything about work horses like those he was driving. He said he had a lifetime of experience with them. I asked if he could stop at a place that sold horses and in the event that I bought two, could we hitch them to the back of the carriage and take them with us? He said this could be done.

He then took a road leading to the outskirts of the town. We came to a farm where I could see many horses. He told me that this is where the Major was going to get the horses he had promised the Indians. This was useful information. We drove to the house. A man walked up to the carriage and greeted the driver. I was introduced as an official of the Company. I told him what I wanted. I hoped to get horses that could pull a carriage, but were also strong enough for heavy work.

He said he had exactly what I had in mind. We went to a large enclosure, where he had a man rope two horses and bring them to us. My driver looked them over closely. One horse was two years old and the other was three. Both were big, heavy horses and looked to be in good condition. The owner told me he had just bought them from a farmer who had raised them himself. He had used them for both carriage and farm work. His reason for selling them was to get cash for further land purchases. He had many horses.

The driver said they were in excellent condition. I

asked the owner what he wanted for them. He gave me a price that I thought was very high. I talked it over with my driver, who agreed the price was a little too high for them. He said he would talk with the man without my presence to see what could be done. He was successful in getting the price down to what the man had wanted for the horses in the first place. I paid the owner the agreed price. I then paid extra for two bridles and some rope.

After the horses were tied to the back of the carriage, we left for our destination. At the inn during our evening meal the driver told me that he had told the horse dealer I was an important official with the government and could hurt his business with them. This was why he lowered the price as much as he had. I thought I had made a good investment. I would have Slow Bear take the horses to the Durham Post and leave them with Sarah.

The rest of the trip was uneventful. On the eighth day we arrived at the place where I had planned to meet the Major. Mr. Butler and Slow Bear were glad to have me back.

I spent the evening telling them about the property I had bought and about the horses. I asked Mr. Butler and the Major if they would use their influence to see that my bid for the ship would be successful. They both agreed to do all they could. We made plans to continue with our project involving Indian lands. They had been busy during my absence, contacting tribes in the areas they were interested in. Plans were made to go to the Seneca Nation to negotiate with them. As we were to be nearby, I asked if Slow Bear could take my new horses to the Durhams. They agreed.

The area that interested the Major and Mr. Butler included the Wenro group. This was a small band situated between the Erie and the Seneca tribes. They were, however, considered to be part of the Seneca, because they pretty well dominated the Wenro and Erie tribes and were closely related to them. Slow Bear left the next morning with the horses. The rest of us left shortly before noon. As I was familiar with this area, it was decided that we would all arrive at the villages together.

We now made it our practise to call on the individual villages. We had found that meeting with the tribes collectively did not work. Many of them did not want a central group bargaining for them because as a result they received very little of the spoils. So we went from one village to another, at times visiting two in one day. We listened to their stories of mistreatment by the White settlers and tried to smooth things out. We gave the Indians rifles, cloth, horses, and tools to pacify them. Consequently we were successful in our dealings. It was now up to the settlers to be a little more understanding of the Indian's feelings. Years later it was evident to me that our efforts had been wasted. The settlers and their leaders refused to be considerate of the Native people.

Chapter 31
Doing Business
with the White Man

After two months of traveling and negotiating with various tribes, we arrived back at the Durham Trading Post. Sarah and I were happy to be together again. Slow Bear had kept busy gathering hay for the winter. Using the two horses I had bought recently and Fish Head's help, a good supply of firewood had been gathered for the Post. Mrs. Durham and Sarah had collected berries and nuts and had dried venison and fish they had obtained from the local tribe. Now all was ready for winter.

After visiting with the Durhams for a while, Mr. Butler and the Major left in their carriage, promising to be in touch before spring. They planned to spend the winter months in New Amsterdam. It was still early autumn, so Slow Bear and I decided to go to New Amsterdam too. I wanted to transfer funds to pay for all the things I had purchased. If my bid on the ship was successful I would need the money for its purchase. Sarah had at least two months to wait before our baby would arrive.

With Fish Head's help, Slow Bear and I moved most of my hoard of gold coins from the cave to the Post. We made leather bags to carry the money in. They were made to fit in the saddle bags. We decided to take the two riding horses and one work horse to carry the load. I left enough coins with Sarah to take care of any needs she might have.

It was a clear fall day when we left the Post. I promised to return as soon as possible. We moved steadily along the trail, making very good time. We spent the first night at the inn and were on our way again before daybreak. On the second day it was early afternoon when we passed the inn where we usually stayed. We traveled on, spending the night outdoors. This way our coins would be safe from prying eyes. During the third week of our travels we reached the town of New Amsterdam. We went quickly to our inn for the night.

Early the next morning we went to the office of Arthur Coglin, my lawyer. I left the money with him for safekeeping. He had a large steel vault where he kept important documents, so I knew my gold coins would be safe there.

After discussing the bid on the ship with Mr. Coglin, Slow Bear and I went to call on the Major. He received us with delight and asked why we were in town. I told him about the bid on the ship. He said he would go with me that morning to see the government agent who was in charge of the bidding.

We went to a building near the dock and met a man who was in Army uniform. This was not unusual. Most people connected with the government were Army personnel. He greeted the Major with respect and asked how he could be of service.

The Major told him why we were there and asked if there had been a decision on the bidding. The man said that there were only two bids and they were being processed. He said the Trading Company and one James Durham were the bidders.

The Major then introduced Slow Bear and me. The man showed surprise when he shook my hand. "You have made a very generous bid," he exclaimed, meaning that he wondered if I had the money to pay. I told him I had just that morning deposited ten times that amount of money with my lawyer, whom I named. He knew the lawyer and knew also that I spoke the truth, so he did not have to ask me outright if I had the funds.

After a brief discussion we left the office. The Major said we were near the main office of the Trading Company and suggested we see Mr. Butler. Upon entering the office we were surprised to see Peter Durham at the first desk by the door. We were delighted to see each other and wanted to talk, but the Major asked if we could see Mr. Butler.

Peter left and returned with Mr. Butler. He was surprised to see us. The Major told him why we were there and asked if the Trading Company was really interested in the ship. Mr. Butler had no idea, but said that the man who did know was available to see us. I asked if it was possible for us all to go to lunch and talk there. They thought it was an excellent idea. After being introduced to the Company man we went to a small pub nearby.

We were told the firm called the Northwest Company was not really interested in the ship but wanted to make sure it would not fall into a competitor's hands. We told him that no other company had made a bid. Their bid and mine were the only ones submitted. He showed surprise at this and then inquired my reasons for wanting the ship.

I told him truthfully that the ship would be used to transport goods between the New World and the old. There were many things being produced here, more than just furs and Indian clothing. Lumber and many manufactured products were being developed. There was maple syrup, which was an Indian product, cheese, and wool clothing. There was a market for these in places other than England and we proposed to pursue it.

Everyone listened carefully to what I had to say. When I had finished speaking they agreed there were more products and other markets to be served than those in England. I mentioned that the Caribbean and the southern part of the New World could be explored for future markets. The Major said I would be well advised to stay clear of the Caribbean and southern areas because of the prevalence of pirates who were becoming most bothersome.

The local manager of the Trading Company said he would need to look into abandoning their bid for the ship and would write for advice from London. It would take about three weeks before he had an answer and to check with him at that time. He returned to his office. Slow Bear went back to the inn. The Major, Mr. Butler, and I went to the ship that I had bid on.

They looked the ship over and agreed it was still a good vessel. After saying goodbye to them I went looking for the Captain who was to be my partner. I found him in the drinking establishment I knew he frequented. When I had filled him in on what I had done that day he was pleased. He was also pulling strings to help our bid to be accepted. He talked about what we would do if we were able to get the ship. He outlined some plans he had.

He wanted to take lumber and other products to England, then return with tools, tea, spices, and animals for the New World, as well as passengers. He wanted to go to the Caribbean for sugar, molasses, and rum. These products he would take to the Old World. He knew this would take capital. Perhaps we could get a line of credit here in New Amsterdam. Immediately, I saw an opportunity where I could make more money, without the Captain being aware of it. If I supplied the financing without his knowledge, then I could claim a greater share of our profits. I made a mental note to discuss this with my lawyer.

The next morning, while Slow Bear readied the animals for our return home, I called at the office of Arthur Coglin. I told him everything that had transpired the previous day. I mentioned the financing of our cargoes. He said he would make the necessary arrangements and keep them secret from everybody. He asked if he could participate in the venture. I assured him I would be happy for him to do so. I told him that I must return home for a few months because of my family. I asked him to get a message to me if he heard anything in regard to my business ventures. He assured me he would.

Chapter 32
I Become a Father

Slow Bear and I left for home. The trip was uneventful. After three weeks of travel we arrived at the Durhams' place, which was no longer an active Trading Post. There were many White families settling nearby. It made the Durhams happy to have their own kind as neighbours.

Sarah was glad to see me return and demanded that this time I stay. Fish Head was like a child as he looked through our luggage for anything we may have brought for him. As usual the Durhams were happy to see us. Suddenly, I realized how much older they looked. They were now retired and making plans to move to New Amsterdam to be close to Peter. So far he had not found suitable accommodation for the three of them.

Mrs. Durham was in no hurry to leave, however. She wanted to be here when the baby was born. Sarah was due to have the child any time now. She had made arrangements for an Indian lady to be here with her all the time, just in case. This was a pleasant woman, somewhere in her forties. She had many children of her own and for years had acted as a midwife in the tribe.

To an Indian woman, giving birth was not a complicated matter. Usually she would be alone when it happened. Sometimes during the summer months she would be with her man on a hunting expedition. When she gave birth in the village there were relatives or a midwife who would help. The father was usually banned from this process, even when there were just the two of them present. Many times a man would leave camp in the morning and come home in the evening to find his woman nursing a newborn child.

Death of the mother or child during the birth was rare, but later the child could become ill and die. Since the White Man had come to our country, the disease they had brought with them often attacked the very young and killed them. It seemed that older people had built up an immunity to some of the diseases. During an epidemic they would escape unharmed, only to die a few years later of the same disease that had caused the epidemic. We were never sure who was safe.

Mrs. Durham and the Indian midwife were agreeable on most things, but they argued about cleanliness. Mrs. Durham made sure that everything was clean and sterilized. The midwife did not agree with this approach.

Nevertheless, Mrs. Durham had her way. I am sure that Sarah was responsible for that. I, for once, had no say in the matter, so I kept my mouth shut as I had been instructed to do. I was told I had done all the damage I was going to do. I was banished to the barn with Fish Head, Slow bear, and the four horses.

One morning I was awakened by the crying of a baby. This is how I found out I was a father. Quickly I pulled on my clothes amid the confusion as Slow Bear and Fish Head did the same. We stumbled from the barn into the sunshine, still pulling on our clothes, and rushed to the house. Mrs. Durham met me at the door holding a baby wrapped in a blanket. I pushed past her to get to Sarah. She was sitting up, looked worn out and tired. I gathered her into my arms and held her.

She asked me what I thought of our daughter. I said I had not taken the time to look at her, or even ask what sex it was. Mrs. Durham entered the room with the baby and put her in Sarah's arms. She pulled back the blanket. I looked at a replica of Sarah . . . the same big eyes and pale skin. What a beauty she was. Sarah handed the baby to me. I took her out to show Slow Bear and Fish

Head. They were ecstatic when they saw her. Fish Head was puzzled, but Slow Bear was so happy, one would think he was the father.

The baby started to cry so I returned her to Sarah. The Indian midwife then took her and performed some kind of ritual that was necessary for the newborn. Mrs. Durham looked on in disapproval. Sarah showed no concern, so I had none. I left the room so they could quiet the baby and to let Sarah rest. Mrs. Durham and the midwife were also tired.

When I went outside, Slow Bear was trying to make Fish Head understand where the baby had come from, but he was not successful. He asked me if he could go to our mother's village to spread the happy news. I agreed he should. During the past few months I had noticed that Slow Bear was making every excuse he could to go to our village. I had wondered what the reason for this was, but had been very busy and put it out of my mind.

I tried my best to explain to Fish Head where the baby had come from, but when I was through he had no more idea than when I started. He did understand that the baby had been in Sarah's stomach, but there his reasoning came to a halt.

That evening Sarah came to the table for our evening meal with the baby. Mrs. Durham claimed that it was too early for Sarah to be up, but the Indian woman said that this was the custom of her tribe. It appeared that Indian women took birth as just a small inconvenience in the day's work. In England women were more pampered than those in the Colony.

But I had seen colonist women go about their daily tasks right after giving birth, too. So it appeared they were getting toughened up by the hard life here.

Sarah placed the baby in a basket while she ate her meal. We were all surprised to see Fish Head go over to the basket. It was unusual for him to leave food untouched. He sat down beside the basket and examined the baby. He opened its covering and looked at the naked child. He then took the child in one of his immense hands to look it over more closely. Mrs. Durham made a move as if to interfere, but Sarah held her arm and told her to wait.

With one huge finger he touched the baby's hand and she grabbed hold of it. He smiled from ear to ear. Very gently he took his finger and stroked her head. He was mumbling something that could not be understood, but the baby seemed to understand him and gave him the first smile I had seen. Sarah went over and stood beside Fish Head with her hand on his shoulder. He looked up at her and said, "You made baby in stomach?" More of a statement than a question.

Sarah replied, "Yes, you could put it that way." He still looked puzzled, but accepted what he was told. He continued to look the baby over until she became restless and started to squirm.

"The baby is hungry and must be fed," said Sarah, and took the baby from Fish Head. He watched as she sat down with the baby, cradling its head in her arms. She lowered her dress and the baby attached itself to her breast.

Fish Head was amazed and exclaimed, "Baby eat you!" Everyone laughed at this.

Sarah said, "No, the baby is getting milk from me. This is what a baby lives on until it is old enough to eat on its own."

Fish Head, while still puzzled, watched as the baby sucked on Sarah's nipple. He said, looking at his own breast, "I feed baby too." This brought more laughter from everyone. Sarah had to explain that only mothers could feed a baby. I could see that he was thinking very hard about this

Mr. Durham, who had been sitting at the table having his usual after-meal pipe, got up and took Fish Head outside with him. Later, I was to learn that he took Fish Head to a White colonist neighbour who had a cow which had just given birth to a calf. He tried to show Fish Head what birthing was all about. This seemed to work because he never asked us again how the baby came to be. He just doted on Sarah and the baby.

Chapter 33
Slow Bear Falls in Love

Slow Bear had not returned and I was getting concerned about him. Sarah shared this concern and suggested that I set out to see what had happened to him. I had planned to take Sarah and the baby to see my mother as soon as the baby was able to travel, but it was still too soon. It was decided that I would go alone.

The next morning I saddled my horse and with a few belongings left the Post. I traveled light so I could make good time. I wanted to return as soon as I found out what was keeping Slow Bear. The trails through the forest were well-used now, so it was no trouble finding the shortest route to our mother's village. It took me four days to get there. Mother and I were happy to be together again.

She wanted to know all about the baby, so it was some time before I could question her about Slow Bear. I could see she was hesitant to talk about him, but I persisted. Finally, she told me that he was in love with a girl in the next lodge. I said I thought this was great news. But she told me there was more to it than that.

The girl, now eighteen, had been married to a young man. Shortly after their marriage he had gone to battle with the English against the French. The country was now in a stage of "all out" war between the English and French. Unfortunately, the young man had been killed by a Frenchman. Under the custom of the tribe, the girl was given to the young man's older brother.

This did not please the young girl, nor the wife of the brother. Because of this, the girl asked for and received the protection of the Clan Mother until the problem was settled by the Chiefs. The older brother could, if he wished, cancel the custom and allow the girl her freedom. But this he refused to do. So the Chiefs were to settle the matter.

Since Mother was the Clan Mother of her lodge, she was a good friend of the Clan Mother who sheltered the girl. It was when they were together in the company of the young girl that Slow Bear met her. He was instantly smitten and asked Mother to arrange for him to marry the girl. This she could not do. So Slow Bear approached the older brother, but instead of negotiating an agreement, the meeting ended in a violent argument.

Slow Bear, therefore, was told he could not to go near the girl. He was not allowed within the palisades of the village. I asked my mother where I could find him. She directed me to an old campsite outside the village. I went there immediately. Slow Bear was surly and in a foul humor when I found him. I questioned him about his problem and he told me he would handle it himself.

I could see he was very upset, so I sat quietly and listened as he told me of all he planned to do to the older brother. I told him to quiet down and stop acting foolish. He got angry and walked into the bush in a huff. I sat by the fire for over two hours before he returned. He sat down, saying nothing.

Finally, I said to him, "Little Brother, we have been through much together. But we have always come through by working side by side. I am sure we can get through this problem too, but not by acting violently. We must attack this man in his weakest spot and if you will give me a chance, I will find it."

He sat silently for a while, then said, "You are the older brother and have proved your wisdom to me many times in the past, so I will put my trust in you."

Having said this, he went to his furs and slept soundly. It was as though a heavy burden had been taken from his shoulders. I sat there for hours thinking of the best way to approach this problem. I was beginning to wonder if it could be solved. I finally slept where I sat and awakened the next morning feeling stiff and cold.

Soon, Slow Bear had the fire going again and made a hot meal for us. I told him the key to settling his problem was the older brother. The Chief was not about to break custom just so he and the girl could marry. I said I would contact the brother and try to come to some agreement, no matter the cost. He seemed willing to have me do this.

After we had eaten I went back to the village. I asked our mother if I could talk with the older brother. Although she was not sure if he would see me, she said she would try to arrange something with her friend, his Clan Mother.

It took two days of waiting before she had a reply. He consented to see me, but wanted two of his friends to be present for his protection. He did not want a re-occurrence of what he had received from Slow Bear.

The meeting was set for the following afternoon. I was first to arrive. He came with two friends with him. He introduced them and then himself. I began the conversation by saying how sorry I was that he had lost his younger brother. I offered my sorrow at his family's grief. I told him that he was to be congratulated on observing the customs of his tribe and for doing his duty in memory of his lost brother.

My approach seemed to be having the desired effect. He smiled and became more friendly. His two companions were also relieved, perhaps because they could see there was going to be no fighting. I told him that I apologized for the actions of my brother, but he was young and not as mature and knowledgeable as we were. He accepted the apology and made a remark about foolish young people in love.

He was honest with me, stating that his wife was not happy about his having a younger woman in the lodge and about him having to plant his seed within her, as was the custom. He had three children, a wife, and an old mother to care for and did not need additional problems. Another woman and more children did not please him.

But, he added, "Custom is custom," and he was willing to abide by it. I told him I was sympathetic to his problem. I said also that I would like to help him to be free of it with a handsome profit for himself. He paid attention immediately when I mentioned profit and wanted to know what I had to offer. I told him I would give him a very fine horse if he would decline the custom. He thought about this, then said he wanted two horses and two rifles.

I was shaken by this. I knew I could not, even for Slow Bear, pay such a price. I told him it was out of the question. He then started to complain that his younger brother had gotten him into this mess. I told him that his younger brother was not to blame, but the Frenchman who killed him. He then went into a long talk of what he would do if he met a Frenchman.

It was then that a thought struck me. I told him Slow Bear and I had successfully fought the French. I went into the whole story of our conflicts with the French. I told him that Slow Bear had killed a French officer, that he even had the sword, gloves, and boots the Frenchman had on him when he killed him. The man said he would like to see them.

It was then I told him that Slow Bear would gladly give them to him as something to remember his younger brother by. Again, I made an offer of a good horse and a rifle, if he would decline the custom. This time he discussed the offer with his friends. Finally he agreed. He asked that he be given the articles of the Frenchman before he declined the custom. I said, "Of course," knowing they were with my mother in her lodge.

We parted in a friendly manner. I made haste to get to my mother's place and have the articles sent to him.

They were in his possession within the hour and the deal was sealed. He went directly to the Chief and declined the custom. The Chief then advised my mother that Slow Bear could enter the village once again. I went to Slow Bear and told him everything that had happened. He was delighted, to say the least. He questioned me about the articles I claimed he had taken from a French officer he had killed. He said he could not remember killing a French officer and taking these things. I laughed and told him I had taken them from a drunken Indian after one of our battles and I never knew the Frenchman either. We both laughed about this.

The rifle we had, but had to get a horse from somewhere. That night we rode to the closest White village. We bargained for a horse that was getting a little too old for much use, and the price was right. We had an old saddle and bridle thrown in. On our return to our mother's village, Slow Bear took the horse, rifle, and gear to the older brother. He was very happy.

Arrangements were made for Slow Bear and the girl to become man and woman. Her name was Many Leaves. She was very pretty, with a ready smile and a great sense of humor. She was small and inclined to be thin. She and Slow Bear were very much in love and we were all happy for them. Two days later the ceremony took place. It was quite similar to the one which Sarah and I had performed when we were made man and woman.

Three days later I took my leave. Slow Bear and his new woman agreed to meet me at the Post within a few days. Many Leaves had things to do with family and relatives before she could leave the village. My mother and her friend the Clan Mother felt somehow that their lodges had become joined by the marriage.

It again took me four days to arrive at the Post. I was glad to see my new baby and Sarah again. What a beauty my little baby was with her dark hair and blue eyes. She was always happy and smiling. Who would not be with two doting mothers to care for her every wish. Mrs. Durham considered her to be her grandchild and sat for hours holding her. I told them all the details of Slow Bear and Many Leaves. They were happy for them and looked forward to meeting Slow Bear's new woman. They arrived six days later. Sarah and Many Leaves became instant friends.

After things had settled down, I began to take an interest in the Post again. It was a nice place to be, but I knew one could not make a living here. It was not a Trading Post any longer and even though the buildings were good, there was only a small area to farm. I spoke with the Durhams. I suggested that perhaps they would like me to build a house for them on the land I now owned in New Amsterdam.

I told them that I intended to build a home there for Sarah and myself as soon as possible. They were delighted with the idea. It especially appealed to them because they could be with Sarah and me, and also with Peter. I talked this over with Sarah. She was pleased that the Durhams could live near us for she was very fond of them. They were like parents to us both.

Chapter 34
I Return to New Amsterdam

A week later, word came from Arthur Coglin, my lawyer, that the bid for the ship was soon to be announced and I should make myself available for it. I discussed this with Sarah. Although we were both loathe to part, we knew it was something we had to do. I told the Durhams I would start the cottage for them when I arrived in New Amsterdam.

It was difficult to get Slow Bear to leave Many Leaves, but they both realized the importance of getting our business taken care of. We left the next morning with our horses, promising to return as soon as we could. Neither Slow Bear nor I was happy about having to leave. It took us three weeks to get to our inn in New Amsterdam. During this time we were amazed at the number of Whites who were now in the region.

The encroachment of the Whites on Indian lands was slow and methodical. Where there was an Indian village, they took the land around it, until it was completely surrounded. This made the Indians, who were raised in a communal setting, feel separated from their own kind, very vulnerable and isolated. They would abandon the village and move out, leaving their land to the White people. This was happening all the time.

I contacted my lawyer the next morning and made an appointment to see him the following day. That afternoon I went to a carpenter's shop. I asked about building a cottage on my land. We went to the property in a wagon, and they did a quick survey of where the cottage could best be built. We picked a place on a small rise that gave a nice view of the river. There was good garden soil behind where the house would be built. I told them I wanted two bedrooms, a large kitchen, and a small parlor with a stone fireplace at the end. They were to give me an estimate in two days.

Early the next morning I went to see my lawyer. He was convinced that my bid for the ship was going to be accepted. I told him that I was going to Albany that afternoon to see how my lumber and raft-building businesses were doing. I mentioned the cottage I was building for the Durhams. After I left him I walked to the Company office where Peter worked. We had lunch together so I could fill him in on all the news. He was particularly pleased that I was building a home for his parents.

I returned to the inn and asked Slow Bear to prepare the horses for our trip to Albany. We then left New Amsterdam, arriving in Albany two days later.

Immediately upon arrival, I went to the riverside to see John Coolidge, my partner who was the shipbuilder. He was happy to see me and gave me a tour of his yard. The barge, or I should say raft, that he had been building was now operating between the two shores of the river. This was the only way to travel from shore to shore, unless you liked to swim. The raft was making a good profit and was kept busy morning to night. He had hired a crew to handle this enterprise.

He was working on a second raft and hoped to start a third one soon. Business was brisk and he was pleased with our arrangement. He told me that my lawyer, Mr. Coglin, had been in touch with him about doing the accounting. He was happy with that.

When I left John Coolidge, I took the raft across the river and went to the lumber camp that I had heavily invested in. My partner there was Burt Seagram. He too, was glad to see me. He said he had received the items I had shipped to him from the ironmonger. He wanted more of the same and asked if I would take care of it. I told him I would attend to it as soon as I returned.

There were piles of logs everywhere. He had ten crews of two men each, sawing the logs into planks. This was a long, tedious process. The log was winched onto a frame that was built above the ground. One man stood on the platform on top of the log, while the other stood below. Between them they pulled and pushed a long saw along the log to cut planks, at the same time trying to cut each plank into a uniform thickness. They also cut heavier timber for other uses. What the lumber was to be used for determined the thickness of the plank.

In the river, logs were chained together to make a large boom. These were floated to a mill in New Amsterdam, or loaded onto ships for England. I was altogether pleased at with what my partner had accomplished. He too told me he had heard from Mr. Coglin, my lawyer, about doing the accounting for the company and was glad to have this arrangement.

I asked him about starting a mill in my area and told him of the land I had purchased. He asked me if there was a stream on the property. I told him I had not noticed. He said he would come down the following week so we could look over the land together.

I again crossed the river by raft to the village. I was in time to have an evening meal with Slow Bear. During the meal I filled him in on my day's activities. He had wandered around the village. We spent the night at a small inn on the outskirts of the village. The next morning we left for New Amsterdam and arrived two days later. At the inn, a message was waiting for me to get in touch with the carpenters about the house I was going to build.

Slow Bear and I went to the carpentry shop. We were invited to the owner's house for tea. The estimate he gave me was quite expensive, so I asked if he could do any better. He told me the cost of the materials was the most expensive part of the estimate. I asked him if I were to supply all the lumber, could he lower the estimate? He said it would cut the cost to less than half. I asked him to prepare a list of what lumber was required and I would see what I could do.

Slow Bear and I went to my property and looked it over to see if there was a stream running through it. There was not. We went to a land agent in town who told me of several pieces of land he had for sale. I told him I wanted a piece of property for a lumber mill but it had to have a stream running through it. Immediately, he told me of a piece of shoreline property that was about five miles upstream from where my property was. It had a fast-moving stream on it. He warned me that the shoreline was swampy and the river in front of the property was shallow.

The next day, Slow Bear and I went to see this piece of land. We found a fisherman who took us along the river. We spent three hours looking it over and returned too late to see the agent. The next morning I went to see him. He told me what was being asked for the land, which, by the way, was about three hundred and ten acres. I made him an offer for less than half of what the owner was asking, pointing out that it had a poor shoreline, was on the wrong side of the river, and would not make good farm land.

He contacted the man who owned the property. Surprisingly, he agreed on my price. At that time, most of the land was given to men who had served in the Army. They were issued a section by the Crown as a reward for their service. They did not have their choice of land, but had to take what was available at the time they applied for it. Naturally, politics were involved. If the man was an officer, or knew someone who was important, he was given the best piece of land that was available. It was stipulated that he must do something with the land before he was given title. In this case, the man had thrown up a log shack, so he had the title to the property.

Most of the time the men did not intend to stay on the land. They just wanted to get it to sell and return to England. That is why I was able to purchase this section for such a ridiculously low price. There were no restrictions on how I, as a second owner, could use the land. It could be used for any purpose I wanted. It could be farmed, used for commercial purposes, subdivided and sections sold, or just left to sit. This piece of land still had virgin forest on it, so it did have some value, but not much. There were trees for the taking everywhere.

When I told Slow Bear the arrangement I had made, he laughed at me. He said it was strange that an Indian had to buy the land that we already owned. I could see his point, but reminded him that as a White man doing business in their world, I had no choice. As an Indian, I would not have taken that piece of land as a gift. We both agreed on that. He said he knew of a few swamps he would be glad to sell me. We both laughed at this. I was happy with the deal and hoped my partner, Mr. Seagram, would agree.

The next morning I went to see Mr. Coglin and had him finalize the deal on the property. He had not heard official word yet on the ship, but felt confident. He told me that a line of credit would be no problem for our cargo. He advised me that with so many business interests in and around the area, it would be to my advantage to settle here. I told him I was about to do something about that, but wanted to have a home built for the Durhams first.

The next day, Mr. Seagram arrived and we spent the day looking over the property that I had just purchased. He thought it would do very nicely. We made plans as to where we could create a small dam for water to turn the waterwheel. This was necessary to have power to operate the saw in order to cut the lumber. It was intended to make lumber by a less "labor intensive" way. He would send men down next week to start clearing our land of useful trees. A small landing that would take one of our rafts could be built at the mouth of the stream.

I liked the progressive and aggressive way this man worked and knew he was the best partner I could have found. I gave him the list of material from the carpenter and told him it would cost me less than half if I supplied my own lumber for the house. He said he would get a raft from my other partner and load it with lumber. I could store the surplus on my property near town and sell it from there. In other words, I would have a lumber yard from which to sell locally and also ship to England if I was successful in my bid on the ship. This certainly appealed to me.

Chapter 35
I Own a Ship

A few days later, I received a message from my lawyer asking me to attend a meeting in his office the following day. I was certain it was about my bid for the ship. I made sure I was present at the time specified in the message.

When I arrived, I was surprised to see Mr. Butler, the Major, the man from the Trading Company, and two other gentlemen seated in Mr. Coglin's office. They were introduced as the people handling the sale of the ship for the Crown.

One of the men representing the Crown announced that the bid by Mr. James Durham had been accepted, but there were some formalities to be taken care of. This was why these people were present. They wanted assurances about my reasons for wanting the ship.

I told them it was strictly for commercial purposes. It would be operating between the Colony and our Mother Country and would be subject to His Majesty at all times. I further stated that it would be registered with the British Admiralty and made available to them whenever they required it.

This seemed to please the officials immensely. I could tell that my lawyer, Mr. Butler, and the Major were also pleased with my statement. They were in turn questioned about my affairs and my loyalty. When the questioning was finished and the official reassured, they stated that all was well. Mr. Coglin informed them that he would come to their office later that afternoon with the funds to complete the deal.

I immediately asked all attending to have lunch with me at the nearest inn. They accepted. Mr. Coglin and the officials left as soon as they had finished eating, but Mr. Butler and the Major stayed on. We talked over a few pints of ale. By the time I returned to my lodging it was late afternoon. Slow Bear was anxious to hear the news and he was delighted with what I had to tell him.

The next morning I made arrangements to have the ship brought to a public dock. I wasted no time in hiring the people I would need to restore it and make it sea-worthy. The carpenter I had hired to build the home for the Durhams had nearly completed the job and had started building a dock on my property. He said he would take care of the woodwork that needed to be done on the ship and that he would hire tradespeople for the rest of the work, which pleased me. I knew I had found the right man to take care of this enterprise.

My partner, Captain Stead, was at sea and not ex-pected back for two weeks. This gave me time to com-plete some of the work necessary. I was anxious for the ship to be in service. A ship in dock made no money. In the meantime, I made several visits to my lawyer regarding a line of credit for the cargo we would be shipping to the Old Country and for that which would be purchased to bring back to the Colonies. Mr. Coglin wanted to invest in it as well as Mr. Butler. So, with three investors, we managed to cover the cargoes' costs and the necessary insurance.

I went to the Trading Company office and spoke with Peter. I asked him if he would like to work for my Com-pany. He readily agreed. He said that he was going to live with his parents and the arrangement would be con-venient for him. I told him that I was building a ware-house and a dock for the ship. There would be an office for him attached to the warehouse where he would man-age the whole operation. I mentioned the lumber storage that was to be nearby. Peter was pleased with his new job.

Burt Seagram arrived the next day. I took him to the property upstream that we had just purchased. He walked over it again and said it would do nicely. We planned where the mill would be located, as well as the dock where the barge would load the lumber to take to our yard downstream. He said he would gather a crew of men right away to start cutting logs in the bush at the back of the property. The logs would be used for the buildings and to build a dam across the stream.

Mr. Seagram said he would work with the carpenter I already had working for me to build the mill and the waterwheels. After the stream was dammed, it would be necessary to build a channel so water could flow past the wheel in order to turn it. The channel was to be controlled by gates. The building was to have a roof, but would be open on all sides.

The machinery consisted of a complicated set of shafts, wheels, and gears which were all made of wood, but reinforced with metal gussets placed and bolted at the joints. This construction would make the saw go up and down against the log, which was on a track moving against the blade. This contraption was called a donkey. The whole thing replaced the two men on the saw blade and was more efficient, as it moved continually. Only one man was needed to sharpen and set the saws and to keep the gears greased.

It would take some time for this operation to be productive, so for the time being he would continue working with the mill in Albany. Nevertheless, we would require logs from this source in the future. Seagram said that one day in the future he would build a home on the property for himself and his family, but not too close to the mill. He told me his family enjoyed being more or less isolated from their neighbours.

Chapter 36
We Move to the City

When I returned to the inn, I informed Slow Bear of the business I had accomplished. I told him we would be returning to the Durham Post the next day. He was to get the horses ready to leave by noon. He was happy to hear this.

The next morning I went to Mr. Coglin's office to tell him I was moving my family to New Amsterdam and would be living in the Durham home until my own was built. He was glad I had made this decision. He promised to monitor the progress on the ship while I was away.

Slow Bear and I left the village. We went to see the horse dealer that I had done business with before. I asked for a team of good wagon horses and a wagon with harness. He said he had just the thing for me. A farmer had asked him to sell a team of horses for him because he had fallen on hard times. The horse dealer said it was an excellent team.

I looked at the horses. They were about nine years old and looked fit and strong. I accepted the dealer's price. He gave me a good price on a rebuilt wagon that had been fitted with new wheels. He had plenty of harness for me to choose from. After paying for my purchases, Slow Bear and I continued on our way with the wagon and team. I had also bought hay, which we put in the wagon. This would feed the animals until we got back to the village.

I tied my horse to the back of the wagon and drove the team. Slow Bear was happy with this arrangement. I was too, because long days in the saddle made me

Sarah and Two Faces

sore and stiff. On the wagon I could get comfortable and even doze when I wanted to. It took us thirty days to arrive at the Durhams and we were all happy to see each other.

When the family realized we were moving, there was a frenzy of activity to prepare and pack. The Durhams had more possessions than the rest of us and almost filled one wagon. I rented the Post to a settler that was new to the area. He was going to farm. The buildings were just what he required, so a good deal was made with him. A few years later he asked to purchase the property and we arrived at a fair price.

In about nine days' time, all was ready to leave the Post. There were sad goodbyes to many Indian neighbours that we had come to know. The Durhams felt sorry to leave the home they had for so many years, but they looked forward to the new location with excitement and a feeling of adventure. With two wagons and a carriage loaded down with all our worldly possessions, we left for New Amsterdam.

It took forty days of slow travel to arrive at our new home. The Durhams were very pleased with the house I had built for them. However, it was going to be a few weeks before they could have it to themselves. Slow Bear and Many Leaves, with Fish Head helping, built a lodge near a lake behind the Durham place. It took them five days to build it.

Sarah and Many Leaves picked the spot for our home, which was just a few hundred feet from the Durhams' place. My partner had been cutting logs in the forest at the back of my property, so the logs were ready for the men to start to build. The carpenter put a crew to work on the house the week after we arrived. It took a further three weeks to have the building to a stage where it was suitable for us to move in.

The woodworkers continued building the warehouse behind the dock. It was now almost completed. I had requested that they build a barn near our house for our animals. This was to stable the horses and the cattle we intended to buy. Mr. Durham and Slow Bear, with the help of Fish Head, intended to start farming. I felt this was an excellent idea and would make us self-sufficient.

Later on we built a carriage house behind our homes and of course there was an outhouse behind each dwelling. These things were added over the following months. With the help of the horses, the land that had been logged was cleared of stumps. A meadow was created and a place to plant hay for winter use. The barn had a loft where we stored the hay. There were other small buildings put up for chickens, geese, and turkeys. There were pig and sheep pens.

Fish Head was really involved with the animals, who seemed to return the affection he showed them. He slept in the barn with them and had a name for every one of them. He and Mr. Durham cared for them. The horses that belonged to my company were kept and cared for near the warehouse building. They pastured with our own horses in the field in front of our home.

Chapter 37
Our Business Booms

While I was relocating my family, the ship had been finished and completely refitted. When Captain Stead returned it was ready for sea. A cargo was quickly assembled and the supplies loaded. A crew was hired and a First Mate chosen. He had been recommended by Mr. Butler because of his experience. It was said that this man had served on a pirate ship at one time. The Captain felt this experience might be useful later on. It proved to be so.

The lumber mill was nearing completion too, and a good supply of logs had already been cut and piled ready for use. We had purchased several teams of horses for the bush work. They were used to pull the logs from the forest. The dam and water channel were now finished. Only the waterwheel and mechanism needed to be completed.

Lumber from the mill near Albany was arriving daily. It was stored beside the ship's dock. We had no difficulty securing other investors. This was fortunate, because my supply of funds was dangerously low. As time went on I stayed more in the background, while my lawyer and Mr. Butler, who was now the general manager, took care of most of the business.

There was now such a large White population in the city that an Indian was rarely seen. If one was, he was a curiosity to some of the people, because they had not come in contact with any Indians since arriving here. Slow Bear and Many Leaves never went to town because of the stares and insults from town people. They would wear only Indian clothes, so they stood out from the others.

The Whites who were our customers wanted to deal only with their kind, so I stayed in the background. I was never told to do this, but it was obvious to me that they preferred to deal with Mr. Butler rather than with me. It was of no big concern to me; I was used to being insulted by both the Indians and the Whites. It was because I was neither one nor the other, but a half-breed.

I did not care what they thought as long as they kept making me rich. My lawyer Mr. Coglin and I would laugh at the people in his office, when they met me for the first time. They would stare and then become un-comfortable. This unbalanced their business judgment. Thinking I was just another dumb Indian, they believed they could take advantage of me. Later, they would be surprised to learn that they were the ones that had been taken advantage of.

This was particularly true in my land deals. I pur-chased the land which surrounded the two sections I already owned. The owners of these tracts of land knew they were unsuitable for farming, and so believed they were selling me useless land. What made them think I was a farmer? I had no interest in the land itself, but realized its location would make it valuable at a future time. This proved to be the case.

My piece of land was near the mouth of the Hudson River where it emptied into the ocean. The water was deep enough for any ship and was on the south shore where a large commercial district was growing. This was reason enough to make it valuable. Having two sec-tions of land on the water and two behind was a good investment. Mr. Coglin invested along with me by taking two sections upriver from my property.

The mill was located five miles upstream on the north shore. I convinced Mr. Coolidge to relocate our boat-building business to alongside the mill in order for it to expand. It was no problem to come downstream from Albany, but it was next to impossible to go upstream. In this new location Mr. Coolidge began building heavy wagons, which were in great demand for hauling. Roads were now leading out from the city to other villages. The people required goods that they could not supply for themselves to be brought from the Old Country.

Our ship brought in much of what filled these needs. On the return trips, products that had been made here were loaded and taken back to the Old Country. Along with lumber and logs, the most popular items were skins and leather clothing. Once in a while our ship would make a trip to Cuba to buy casks of rum. Some of this cargo was unloaded here, but most of it also went to the Old Country. This is where our Mate came in handy. He was familiar with the Caribbean and knew how to avoid the pirates that were numerous there.

On one trip they went to St. Augustine, which I understood to be south of where we lived. Here Captain Stead and the Mate made a deal for some Spanish silverware in exchange for rum. They got it from a man whom they believed was a pirate. The man denied that he was. He said that he had bought it from a pirate. There were plates, cups, and goblets, along with pitchers and other food utensils. When I saw the silverware, I knew that I would have to have some for my own table, so I purchased it from the Company.

Sarah was delighted with the silverware. I had to buy a special cupboard to store it in. I found out, however, that the silverware was only something to look at which required polishing all the time. We never used it on the table. Sarah thought it was too beautiful to eat food from.

Chapter 38
We Get a New Church and School

One day Mrs. Durham brought a man to see me. He was introduced as an Anglican minister. They asked if I would donate a small piece of property to build a church on. Because Mrs. Durham had asked, I could not refuse. She and her husband had been more than a mother and father to me.

I chose a half-acre below the Durham home beside the property line. It was above the road that ran across the land about a thousand feet from the water's edge. I agreed to supply the lumber needed for the building, if they supplied volunteer labor to build it, which they did. Later on they added a carriage house and two backhouses.

The minister lived in town nearby, so I did not have to build a home for him. I found out later that when surveying large sections of land, the Crown insisted that a parcel of land be set aside by the land surveyors for the Anglican Church. It was discovered that this had been done, but on my section, next to the one I lived on. I had voluntarily donated the land, so I had the choice of what part to give. If I had not, then they could have made the choice.

Later, I was asked for another piece of land next to the church to be used as a graveyard. I gave them a half-acre of the section next to the church. The White people in the church insisted on dying, so wanted a Christian burial on Christian land. I was not aware that the land I had given them was Christian land. The Durhams were grateful for the church and attended faithfully.

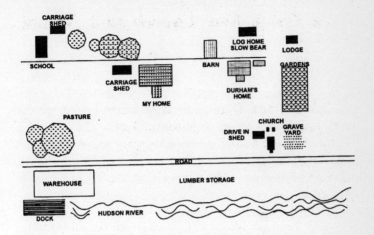

Homesite in New Amsterdam

Every week Mrs. Durham decorated the church with flowers from her garden. With Fish Head's help, she did the cleaning and kept the grounds presentable. Fish Head was given the job of excavating the graves when this became necessary. He was paid a small sum for this work.

As time went on, Mrs. Durham put pressure on Sarah and me to join the church. I was reluctant to do so, but it was made plain to me that as a businessman in the community, it could have its benefits. Therefore, we were baptized and learned the catechism, to become accepted members of the Anglican Church. Slow Bear refused to have anything to do with it. He felt our own religion was adequate and could see no reason to change. I agreed with him.

About a year later I was approached by a group of neighbours to donate land for a school. I hesitated to do this, until Sarah reminded me that in the future our children would need a place to receive their education.

I gave an acre of land from the top of the section we lived on. It was across the property and so away from our home. I supplied the lumber for the one-room building, as I had done before for the church. Volunteers built the structure. They later added a small carriage house and two outhouses. Benches were made for the classroom. Books were gathered from the people in the neighbourhood around us.

When the building was ready, they hired a teacher who had just arrived from England. This man was in his middle twenties with fair hair and an athletic build. It seemed to me that it was not long before all the children were occupied with school work, our own included.

By this time Sarah and I had three children, all daughters. Slow Bear and Many Leaves had two boys. Slow Bear would tease me continually because of my lack of sons. It made no difference to me if I had sons or daughters. Whatever they were, I loved them. But remarks were made about my manhood and that bothered me. Finally, Sarah and I had a son and it was a relief to be free of the comments. As it turned out, we had three daughters, two sons, and finally two more daughters. Slow Bear and Many Leaves had two sons and one daughter.

We had a house full of children and Sarah was kept busy morning to night. We hired a local Indian woman who had no family to live in and assist Sarah with the children. The older girls were a help to their mother.

Chapter 39
Slow Bear Moves

One evening, Slow Bear and Many Leaves came to my home to speak to me. They said they were going to move away to be with her family's tribe so their children could learn Indian ways. After much prying, it was disclosed that their children were the brunt of racist remarks from the White children in the school. I had not thought this would ever happen, considering our position and the fact we had given the land for the school, even though I had personally been subjected to it in my day.

This made me angry and very sorrowful to know that they were leaving us. I tried to think of some way I could get them to stay, but could not come up with any answer. They left us one late summer day and our hearts were heavy. They took one wagon and the team of horses that were his. He tied his saddle horse behind the wagon.

After they left, a terrible loneliness captured us. The Durhams were as sick about it as were we. The teacher and neighbours gave us much sympathy and understanding. They had not known there were racist people in the community. Most of them lived downstream from us. For the next four weeks the minister gave stern lessons in the church about racism. But it was too late . . . Slow Bear was gone.

Around the middle of winter, Sarah, the girls, and I made a trip to visit Slow Bear and his family at their village. We were all very happy to see one another. Many Leaves and her family could not have done more to make us welcome. Slow Bear admitted that he missed their lodge by the lake and often wished they could return. It was during one of these discussions that I finally had an idea to solve the problem.

I asked Slow Bear and Many Leaves if there was anyone in her family that would like to come and live with them to teach their children Indian ways. I told them I would also hire a teacher to educate them privately. They discussed this with her relatives. They found an older gentleman, an uncle who had no family other than Many Leaves. He agreed to come with them.

This made us all very happy. So plans were made for their return in the spring. We left for home in a happier mood than when we had arrived. Immediately upon our arrival at home, I made arrangements to have the carpenter build a log house for Slow Bear and his family. It would face onto the lake and have three bedrooms and a kitchen. Their old lodge would not be far from it, so the uncle could live there.

I told the Durhams about the plan. Mrs. Durham volunteered to teach the children so they would not have to attend the school. The schoolteacher also volunteered to help in any way he could. Fish Head told me he had missed his brother. There were tears in his eyes when he found out they were returning. This man had so much love for us all and we had as much for him.

What a happy day it was when they returned! Everyone was so glad to see them again. Slow Bear was very pleased with his new home. Many Leaves had been asking him for one. They had brought Many Leaves' younger sister with them. She was a pretty girl about fourteen years of age.

We found out that she had accidentally been named Noise of Rain. When she was born, it was raining very hard. The midwife came to her mother and asked, "What is the name of your baby girl?"

Not being able to hear properly because of the rain making so much noise on the roof and being weak from the childbirth, she answered feebly, "I can't hear you . . . noise of the rain."

The midwife heard only the words "Noise of Rain," and mistakenly believed this was the name of the child. She went to the next lodge where the baby was being cleaned by relatives and told them "Noise of Rain." They thought it was a peculiar name for the mother to give a child, but it was her baby and she could give her whatever name she chose. Later, when the mother found out what had happened, it was too late to do anything about it. They called her Rain for short.

Later that summer, Many Leaves' family arrived for a visit. They brought the uncle who would teach the boys Indian ways. He was happy with the lodge that Slow Bear had fixed up for him. The family stayed for over a month. When they prepared to leave, Rain said that she did not want to go back to the village. So they allowed her to stay with her sister. This was a good arrangement because she was a great help to Many Leaves and Sarah.

Chapter 40
Marital Problems

Everything was going along smoothly until one day it was brought to my attention, by a well-meaning neighbour, that my wife Sarah was spending an extraordinary amount of time with the schoolteacher. I was so shocked by what she said that I was speechless. It had never occurred to me that Sarah would be unfaithful. I was aware that I had been, and made the excuse it was the Indian in me.

It occurred to me that Sarah was also part Indian. I made up my mind that I would not cause too much of an uproar if I found the rumor to be true. I would just make sure that the association was ended. I kept an eye on her. She did spend considerable time at the school and in the teacher's company.

A few days later I was approached by the teacher regarding some lumber he required for the school. I told him I had donated all I had intended; anything else would be taken over my dead body. He looked at me in surprise because of the anger in my voice. I think he got my meaning.

Soon after this episode, Sarah suggested that we make some changes in the living room. She wanted to replace the bear skin on the floor with carpet and make a few other changes. I agreed. However, I said, "Do not put anything over the mantle, because I have a fair-haired scalp in mind, that I want to hang there." She turned quickly and looked at me. I knew she understood what I meant by my remark and that I would do what I implied I would do.

Her visits to the school stopped and nothing more was said of the matter. The following spring a woman teacher was hired, as the previous teacher was returning to England. The new teacher was very strict and a real sourpuss, but she was a good teacher.

One day I had just returned from town and gone straight to the barn to unsaddle my horse. Rain came into the barn with Fish Head to collect the eggs, as they did every day. Rain told Fish Head to take the basket to Sarah while she went up to the loft to see if any eggs were there.

In a few minutes Sarah came storming into the barn demanding to know where Rain was. I told her she was up in the loft. She went up the stairs. I heard her give Rain a good talking to and told her to return to the house. A minute later Rain came down the stairs with tears in her eyes and ran to the house. Sarah came down a few moments later. I asked her what was wrong. She said she did not trust me with Rain and that I had better keep my hands off her. I was so surprised that I was speechless.

I agreed that she was a very pretty girl and desirable, but I honestly had no intention of molesting her. In the future, to save myself from Sarah's suspicion, I made certain I was never alone with Rain again. It was later to be that Rain and Peter fell in love and married. The Durhams were happy with their new daughter-in-law and showed her the love they still gave Sarah and me.

Instead of going into the house after I had stabled my horse, I walked over to Slow Bear's home. We talked for a few minutes. I asked them to visit with Sarah and me for a while. Although I did not tell them what had happened, I felt that by having them there it would help to ease the tension a bit. When we arrived at my home everything was quiet. Sarah gave no hint of what had just occurred. Rain was playing with the children and seemed no worse for wear. We sat and talked for some time. The topic of conversation turned to Many Leaves' family. Sarah made mention of how pretty Rain was. We all agreed.

I went over to Many Leaves' chair and putting my arm around her, kissed her on the cheek, saying what a pretty girl she was. She pushed me away playfully and said, "Don't try your stuff on me, you will never have me as long as Slow Bear lives."

I laughed and said, "If that's all it takes, I will have Slow Bear taken care of right away."

We all laughed at this. Sarah said, "He won't do you any good without his balls."

This made us all laugh, but I contemplated the threat and shuddered. After this, Sarah and I understood each other better and our lives were richer because of it.

Chapter 41
Fish Head and the Bear

Fish Head was loved by all who knew him and people tended to forget that he was "slower thinking" than they were. He was still a big lumbering giant of a man and was ever so gentle. He dearly loved the children and animals. He proved this love many times.

One day when I was in the warehouse office discussing some problem with Peter, a noise out by the company barn took our attention. A man ran to us telling me to get over there and save some person from the crazy giant.

Peter and I hurried out. When we entered the barn we saw Fish Head holding a man by his neck against the wall with one hand and threatening him with the other. He was saying in Indian language which the man could not understand, "No hurt my friend!"

I went to Fish Head and attempted to calm him down. There were tears in his eyes and he was very angry. I finally got him to let the man go. It was just in time, as his face was getting purple and he was going limp. He crumbled to the ground. Some men took him to the water pump to revive him.

I asked the men who had witnessed the outburst what had happened. They said the man Fish Head had attacked was having trouble getting one of the horses to accept its harness. He had lost his temper and was whipping the horse when Fish Head came on the scene. He grabbed the man and held him against the wall. I looked at the horse in question and could see the whip marks on its side.

One man said that we should keep that crazy Indian out of the place. I told him immediately that he was fired. I said that Fish Head was my brother and if anyone felt the way this man did, he could leave also. No one did. I explained to them the love that Fish Head had for animals and that he was not as he appeared, a grown man, but a little child. Peter tried to explain that he was mentally retarded, but not stupid and needed their understanding and patience.

One of the men went to Fish Head and, touching his shoulder, said that he was sorry. Fish Head stood up and looked at the man. He apparently liked what he saw, because he engulfed the man in a giant bear hug. Everyone laughed. This broke the tension. Fish Head had made many friends that day.

This gentle giant was continually bringing animals into the barn that had been hurt or injured. There was always something he was nursing back to health, from turtles to snakes, rabbits, and birds; he cared for them all. Our barn was like a zoo. Owls and pigeons lived in the loft. They would sit on his head and shoulders because they knew and trusted him.

He had a mother deer and fawn that would come to him by the lake and eat from his hand. There seemed to be no animal, serpent, or bird around us that did not trust Fish Head. He spent every hour of the day with them, except when Mrs. Durham put him to work at the church.

Unfortunately, it was an animal that nearly killed him. One early spring morning, while chopping firewood for Mrs. Durham, he heard a lamb cry for help. Still holding the axe in his hand, he rushed over to the lake to see what the problem was. He was confronted with a black bear holding a spring lamb that it had just killed.

Not realizing his own danger, he attacked the bear. The bear dropped the lamb and fought back. Although Fish Head hit the bear a hard blow on its head, it still managed to pull Fish Head to the ground and maul him.

Slow Bear was nearby and heard the commotion. He grabbed his rifle and rushed to the scene. He shot the bear, but not before it had seriously mauled Fish Head.

Men came from everywhere and carried Fish Head to the Durhams'. Others saddled horses and raced to town to get a Medicine Man. Slow Bear sent Rain on horseback to bring a Shaman from a nearby tribe. Many Leaves' uncle gave Fish Head first aid as only an Indian could. Doing so probably saved his life.

The Medicine Man from town sewed up the open wounds on Fish Head, but did not feel he would survive. When the Shaman arrived he had the women go to the forest and gather certain plants and roots he required for medicine. For the next four days the Shaman and Many Leaves' uncle sat by Fish Head, performing ceremonies and replacing the herbs that covered his wounds. On the fifth day Fish Head was conscious and wanted to eat. He was allowed only a foul-smelling soupy mixture made by the Shaman.

One peculiar thing that I must mention was information given us by Mrs. Durham. One morning when she went into the bedroom where Fish Head lay unconscious, her attention was drawn to the window. She was surprised to see two owls and several pigeons sitting on the windowsill. To see them there was surprise enough but to see them together was still more amazing.

During the time Fish Head lay in bed, there was always a horse, cow, or some other animal looking in the window of the bedroom. They had never done that before. It was as though they were concerned for their friend who lay on the bed.

The minister and church congregation sent gifts of food to Fish Head and visited him while he was ill. The minister said he had never seen such a gentle man. He recalled that Fish Head always cried whenever a person, stranger or otherwise, was buried in the graveyard. He would keep fresh flowers on the grave for days.

In the meantime, Slow Bear skinned the bear and tanned the hide. He would give it to Fish Head later. He butchered the carcass for meat for us to have for the table. When he presented the bearskin to Fish Head, he was very happy. It became a part of him. He wore it over his shoulders when cold and slept on it at night. He was never without it. It was strange that he appreciated the fur when he loved animals so much. But he considered the bear bad because it had taken one of his lambs.

How happy we were when, except for a few scars, he was fully recovered. He was somewhat of a hero among our close neighbours. But no one was happier than the children, or the animals.

This gentle giant cut quite a figure. He wore large White Man's boots, leather Indian short pants in summer, and White Man's wool pants in winter. He had a black cloth jacket with big brass buttons and braid on the collar and sleeves. He wore a wool shirt in winter, no shirt in summer. But his crowning glory was the old silk top hat that Mr. Durham had given him years before, which he was never without. Now, with the bear fur over his shoulders, he was quite a sight, as you can imagine.

To meet him for the first time could easily make one fearful. Along with his size, with braids down each side of his head and definitely Indian in appearance, he was a daunting figure to come upon.

Chapter 42
A Stowaway

One summer morning, I walked to the warehouse to speak to Peter. The ship had arrived the day before and I wanted to check the manifest with him. The passengers had disembarked on the day of arrival and the cargo was still being unloaded. Many wagons were there being filled up with goods to be delivered to customers in town.

I was at once asked to go on board ship to see Captain Stead, who had left word that he wanted to see me. When I entered his quarters, he, the Mate, and two other crew members were there. Tightly bound on the floor was a Black man. I had never seen a man of this colour before and was surprised. I knew about slavery in the south and the Caribbean, but had not as yet seen any of the people who had been enslaved.

Captain Stead told me that the man had stowed away on the ship when they had loaded rum in Cuba. He had hoped to escape to freedom from slavery in that country. He wanted to return to his home in Africa. I asked if he were a violent man. They said he could not be trusted. I told them to release him from his bonds.

They did as I asked. The Black man stood up and looked at me in fear. I told him no one would hurt him and asked his name. He answered in English, telling me he was named Jim by his masters, but his real name was Konda. I asked him when he had last eaten. He said he had stolen food when in the hold of the ship, but had not eaten for two days.

I ordered that he be fed and given water. He was still very nervous and wanted to escape us if possible. He ate the food he was given. When he had finished I told the Captain that I would take him to my house to question him further. I would let them know what we were to do with him.

Captain Stead and the Mate said that the Black man was a dangerous person and could do me harm if he had the chance. I thanked them and told them I could take care of myself in any event. They also said that the proper authorities should be notified. I told them to hold off until I said so.

I told the Black man what I was planning to do and made him promise not to try to escape. I said he was to be treated as a guest and he should act like one. He had a puzzled look on his face, but said he would behave. I left the ship with him following along beside me. He had tried to walk behind me but I made him do otherwise.

When we reached my house everyone stared at the man because they, like me, had never seen a Black person before. He took their scrutiny in good humor and showed he had good breeding. As my midday dinner was ready, he was invited to join us. He seemed to be confused at our invitation. He was about to decline, when he realized we were treating him as an equal.

During our meal I told him that Sarah and I were of mixed blood, and as a result, did not meet the approval of the White or Indian people. He was amazed at this, because it was evident to him that in this place I had some authority over both races. I told him it was only because it was profitable for them to listen to me.

He was twenty-three years of age and had been captured by White people when he was fourteen. He had been brought by ship to Cuba. There he had been sold to a religious group who grew sugar cane. He said he had not been badly treated as long as he did as he was told. We noticed, however, that he had some lash marks on his back.

He was a strong, well-built young man with short curly hair. It was evident that he was used to hard work.

As far as he was aware, his family was still in his homeland, but so many White people were now raiding their villages that he was not sure. He had met many of his tribe in Cuba who had also been brought in to be used as slaves.

After our dinner, I took him to the lake behind us. There he met Slow Bear and his family. They too were amazed to see a man of his colour. He was just as surprised to see an Indian and to be told that he was my brother. Fish Head came from the barn and was very confused. When he got close to the Black man, he rubbed his skin to see if the black would come off. We laughed at this; even the Black man did.

We introduced Fish Head as our brother also. The Black man looked puzzled. I explained to him that he was not really a blood relative, but that we had adopted him. He could see that Fish Head was mentally retarded. I told him how we had come to have him.

That night the Black man slept in the barn with Fish Head. In the morning he came to our house and asked what was to be done with him. I told him I would help as far as I could, but would not be able to get him directly to his homeland.

Later, I met with the Captain and asked him if he would take our guest to England on his next trip. The Captain wanted nothing to do with the idea, but only to inform the authorities about him. I told him that by doing that, he would have him enslaved again, but this time in another country and I told him I would not stand for that.

We discussed the problem most of the morning, while the Black man sat on the deck awaiting our decision. It was finally agreed that he would work his way aboard our ship to England. There the Captain had a friend who sailed from England to India around the coast of Africa. He would try to make arrangements with his friend to drop the man off on the African coast, as close to his homeland as possible.

If there was a cost to be born for this, I said I would pay it. As far as his being in our country illegally was concerned, it would be canceled as long as he was a member of our crew and stayed aboard the ship. This was agreed upon. We told the Black man our plan. He was happy we would help him. It turned out that he was a good person to have as part of the crew. Captain Stead told me later that he wished he could have kept him on. In fact, the Captain who was to take him to Africa said he would not charge to drop him off, if he proved to be as good a crewman as my Captain said he was.

I often wondered if he made it home again. I hoped so. I heard many horror stories about the Blacks to the south of us who were working on farms. Our ship Captain told us how badly they were being treated. He told us of the horrible conditions they had endured when they were being brought to this country. This made us very sad.

Chapter 43
Trouble at the Mill

Shortly after the episode with the Black man, I was asked to go to the mill. Apparently Mr. Seagram was having difficulties with a tribe of Indians who lived inland, about ten miles from the mill. I could not understand why we would have trouble that far away from the mill.

The following day Slow Bear and I went to the mill. On arrival we met Mr. Seagram and another man. He was an employee of ours that was falling lumber inland. It was explained to me that we cut timber for settlers on their land to clear it for farming. This way we received the timber as payment.

They told me that our timber lots were almost completely cut over and this was the reason why we were now so far inland. The problem that arose with the Indian tribe was over a tree that had been cut by our faller which had killed one of their horses. The Indians claimed that the trees being cut were on their land. I told them that Slow Bear and I would go to the Indian village the following day.

During the remainder of the day Mr. Seagram gave me a tour of the mill. He wanted to show me the improvements that had recently been made in order to improve our production. All the wooden gears and shafts had been replaced with metal ones. The saw blades had been replaced with round blades that cut not only faster, but also more accurately that the old type.

They had extended the mill and installed more saws, so now production was nearly four times what it had been. More men had been hired, meaning a bigger demand for logs. More forest help had also been hired, to cut and haul the trees to the mill. There were piles of lumber everywhere waiting to be barged to our storage area near the ship dock.

I went next door to the mill where the boat and wagon works were. Mr. Coolidge was happy to see me and showed me his plant. They had a dry dock for the boat or barge building. There was a building where they constructed and assembled wagons. The lumber mill next door made it easier for them to get the lumber they required for production. A blacksmith forge had been added. Here they made the steel rims for the wagon wheels and other metal parts they required at both the boat and wagon works and for the mill. My investments were certainly in good hands.

Next day Slow Bear and I saddled up two company riding horses and with a guide left for the Indian village. We arrived late that evening and stayed at the logging camp that night. The next morning, after a light meal, we went to the Indian village. We were met by some young men and taken to the Chief's lodge. When the Chief realized who we were and of our business there, he had the Shaman and Elders summoned to the meeting.

First, they held a small ceremony to ask for blessings for a successful meeting. These were the Wappinger people and they took their ceremonies very seriously. When the sacred firepit was lit, we sat around it in a circle.

I was asked to speak first. I explained that I was here to try to settle the problem arising from a horse being killed by a fallen tree. The Chief spoke, saying that the dead horse was just a minor part of the problem. The encroachment on their lands by White settlers was the main problem and before we could be allowed to continue cutting trees, it had to be settled.

He spoke at great length about how his village was now surrounded by White settlers. They were not being allowed to hunt and fish on these taken lands which had been theirs from ancient times. His people did not have enough land left to grow food and they faced hunger at all times.

While listening to him, I realized I was part of his problem. Earlier, I had participated in the discussions with Major Farnsworth to help the English get permission to have these lands. But the Indians had only agreed to share the lands, not to give them away.

I explained to the Chief and Elders that my only concern was payment for the horse that one of my company employees had accidentally killed. I told them any complaint regarding their land was the responsibility of the Crown and they would have to settle their problems with them.

They asked Slow Bear and me to leave them while they considered my words. I told Slow Bear that I wanted to be alone for a while. I went to a nearby stream to think about the situation and my participation in it years before. I felt responsible in part for the Indian's problem and it bothered me tremendously.

Later, when we were summoned to the circle of Elders and Chief, I was very upset. I really did not want to be there. The Chief spoke first, saying they realized I was in a difficult position, and they did not want to put me there. I interrupted the Chief, telling him it was my fault and not theirs that I was in this position.

I told them I had come prepared to offer horses, rifles, and blankets in return for letting us continue our work. But I knew in my heart that they needed more than that. I said I could tell them that the White Man only wanted to share their land and would offer them farm animals and many other things if they agreed. But they had heard all the White Man's lies before.

I told them that it was the White Man's way to encircle the Indian villages, then force them to leave, because the Indians could not live without their community around them. They had devious ways to make the Indian's life intolerable. I told them that I too had been fooled by the White Man's promises and had become greedy like them. I promised to remove the men that were working on the land next to them and replace the horse that had been killed.

As I talked, I could see the looks of surprise on their faces. Even Slow bear was puzzled. The Chief and Elders asked to be excused and left the circle. Within minutes they were back. The Chief said they believed what I had said and appreciated my honesty. They had agreed that I should let the men continue with their work and the replacement of the horse was accepted.

I told them I would not forget their generosity and thanked them. I said I hoped they would consider moving from the region and find another home more suitable for their needs. They nodded and proceeded with a ceremony of thankfulness. Slow Bear and I left within the hour.

Slow Bear asked if I meant what I said, or was it just a new angle to get them to settle their grievances? I told him I had meant every word of it. He looked satisfied. I knew within myself that I had made a commitment, and that was to never do anything that would harm the Indians again regardless of the cost to me or my company or my White friends.

When we returned to the mill I had Slow Bear pick out the best horse he could find in the stable and have it sent to the tribe. Mr. Seagram was happy the men could start back to work again. He was also happy that replacing the horse was all it cost us.

Slow Bear and I returned to our homes the next morning. I told Sarah all that had happened. She understood my feelings. Later that week I sent a wagon loaded with food and clothing to the tribe as a friendly gift. Again, I realized, this was just to soothe my conscience.

Chapter 44
Things Change, We Do Too

Things went along as usual for the next five years. Our children were becoming young adults. The two older girls were married and living close by. The two boys were finished grade school. They would leave soon to complete their education in England, where I had gone so many years before. Slow Bear had one child at home; two had married and were living in the Indian village of our family.

We were all older, but happy. It was not to stay that way. First, Fish Head became sick. He was ill a year before he finally passed away. The last six months of his life were spent in bed at the Durhams'. Mrs. Durham, now very old, would have no one else nurse him. The doctor advised us that Fish Head suffered from a kidney disease and it was not possible to save him.

We had a Shaman and a Medicine Woman from the local Indian tribe come to see if they could do anything, but he was beyond their help. The Medicine Woman tried many herbal remedies, but none worked. We tried to keep him as comfortable as possible. Near the end, we hired an Indian lady to stay with him during the night, because he needed attention twenty-four hours a day.

He died peacefully one morning. The loss was almost unbearable for everyone. For a while our house was in turmoil. My two sons were preparing to leave the following week for England. The minister of the church, who visited Fish Head daily while he was sick, came to see me the morning after he died.

He seemed very uncomfortable. Finally, I asked him if there was some problem I should know about. He told me that the church people would not let Fish Head be buried in the church graveyard because he was considered a heathen Indian. I was shocked by this news. I, who had given so much to the church, was being refused to allow one of my family to be buried there.

The minister hastened to tell me he disagreed with their decision and would like to conduct the burial service any place else. I believed he was sincere, but told him it did not matter because we were making arrangements for Fish Head to be buried near an Indian village close by. He asked if he could attend the ceremony because he thought very much of Fish Head. I knew this to be true, and consented.

Under the pressure of the time, I did not give too much thought to the church people refusing to allow Fish Head to be buried on church land. Later, this was to occupy my mind and was responsible for my taking a new direction in my life. The day Fish Head was buried, many people arrived to attend the ceremony. Of these were several White people. The Durhams of course were there, along with Mr. and Mrs. Butler, the Seagrams, the Coolidges, my lawyer with his family, and many others.

The funeral ceremony was a very simple one, which consisted of giving back to Mother Earth her son, from whence he had come. Fish Head was dressed in his coat with the brass buttons, wool shirt, and pants. On his head we placed the hat that he had never been without. He was wrapped in the bearskin that he had kept by him always. During the ceremony we thanked Mother Earth for letting him come amongst us, so we could enjoy him. We praised Mother Earth for being so unselfish in sharing one she loved so much. We realized that all people were just a part of her and we were thankful we had a common Mother.

Later, the minister said he had never attended such a beautiful service for the departed. All the people attending had tears in their eyes, Indians and White people alike. Slow Bear and I were particularly sad because we considered him to be a brother to us. Never in my life had I met a man so loving, kind, and considerate of others, as Fish Head had been.

My two boys left for England as planned and we knew they would be gone for at least two years. I hoped they never engaged in business while there as I had done. They had no reason to, for they had sufficient funds for all their needs. Only the younger boy was to return to the New World. The older boy met a girl in England. He fell in love, married, and never came back to see us. I learned that he had gone into his father-in-law's banking business.

Two of the older daughters married White men that lived in the locality. The other girl married a man from further south of us. The two youngest girls were still at home. Later they, too, married White men and lived nearby. Both of Slow Bear's children married into our tribe. This pleased Slow Bear and Many Leaves.

In a few years Mrs. Durham died, followed a few months later by Mr. Durham. They were buried in the churchyard below us. Peter and Rain had three children, all at home at the time. He still worked for my company. Later his son was to join him in the establishment and he and his sisters married locally.

Chapter 45
The Final Changes

Over the years everything changed and so did I. The young man with wide shoulders and narrow waist was now an older man with these dimensions reversed—I now had narrow shoulders and a wide waist. I was fifty-five years of age before I realized it. Slow Bear stayed the same in stature. He was always thin, wiry, and tough as nails. He still lived in the house by the lake. But now, with the children grown and gone, there was only him and Many Leaves. Her uncle then moved into the house with them.

Sarah seemed the same to me, but she too had changed. Having seven children took its toll on her. She still had that beauty about her, but her health had suffered. We lived alone in the big house with a servant girl from the nearby village. We still had horses, but we did not ride. We used a carriage and team instead. Slow Bear still rode his horse and ran the farm.

We closed down the lumber mill, because there was just too much competition now. We sold the building to a man who wanted it for grain grinding. Captain Stead had retired and there was too much competition from bigger companies, so we sold the ship. The purchaser bought the dock and warehouse. Peter continued to work for the new owners.

Mr. Seagram retired and bought more land from me so he could do a little farming, just for something to pass his time. Mr. Coolidge still ran the wagon building business, but had discontinued making barges and boats. This company still made me a little money. I sold most of my land, but kept just enough acreage for a small farm.

When I had bought the land it was extremely cheap, so now the sale of it brought me a good profit. I had no need for more money, so I had no ambition to do anything. I worked with Slow Bear around the farm and the two of us would go fishing in the small lake almost every day. We caught few fish, but it got us out of the house.

In my sixtieth year I lost Sarah, and my world seemed to fall apart. The church people offered to have her buried in the church graveyard, but I refused. We buried her next to Fish Head with the same simple ceremony. I had not expected her to become sick and it seemed to happen overnight. One morning she complained of pain in her lower stomach. The doctor said it was woman's trouble. Two weeks later she was dead. If it had not been for Slow Bear and Many Leaves, I would have died, too.

In a few years I had lost Fish Head, the Durhams, the Butlers, and now Sarah, and my children had all moved away. I would sit on the verandah of my home grieving their loss and feeling sorry for myself. I thought of Sarah and how we had met many years before. I remembered the little waif whom I adopted and her growing up to be such a beautiful woman. I could not forget the spirit she always showed and the love we shared. I would sit for hours with tears running down my cheeks.

I would remember the days spent in this house. Sarah and the girls were continually working on clothes . . . either making new outfits or remaking old ones to fit the younger girls. To me it was a dressmaker's nightmare, as the house was always in turmoil. Many Leaves and her daughter added to the confusion. In the summer we spent hours on the beach by our little lake playing games and swimming. During the cold winter months our spare time was spent indoors. Every Saturday evening was bath time. The day was spent bringing water from the lake which was then heated for our baths. During the week we had a stand-up bath or a good wash.

Because there were nine people in the house, the laundry and ironing was an ongoing chore. During the warm weather Sarah would do these chores in the summer kitchen because it was cooler. It seemed someone was always going to the lake for water, summer and winter. We had to continually gather firewood, which was used for cooking and heating. The laundry iron was heated on the surface of the kitchen stove.

Sarah was the love of my life, but the children received their share of my love too. When they were small they would climb all over me during our play times. I enjoyed these times with my family. All the children loved to ride the horses and swimming seemed to be second nature for them. Slow Bear, our boys, and I spent many happy hours fishing in the lake. At times we would take our sons to the nearby Indian village to enjoy the ceremonies and learn some of the Indian ways.

Day after day I reminisced in this fashion, going over my life and what I had done with it. I felt guilty because I had not done more for my Indian people, but in my heart I knew I had not intentionally hurt them.

I could not say the same for the White people. I had taken advantage of them every chance I got. I had used their women to my own advantage and felt no shame for it, remembering the use the White men made of our unwilling Indian women.

The English had defeated the French and now held most of the territory in the New World. In my own area there were just a few Indians left. I had heard of the Seneca uprising against the Whites.

It was now an oddity to see an Indian in the town. There were many people of mixed race like me. It seemed the Indian blood was being more and more diluted by White blood.

One day, when I was seventy years of age, Many Leaves came running to tell me that Slow Bear had fallen from his horse and needed help. I called two younger men that were nearby and we went to Slow Bear. We found him by the forest near the lake. He was lying beside an outcrop of granite. When we picked him up, I could tell that he was gone. He had hit his head on a stone.

We buried him beside Fish Head and Sarah, leaving room for Many Leaves and me. I moved into the home of Slow Bear with Many Leaves. She asked me to share her home as she did not want to be alone. Her Uncle had died years before. We had separate rooms. There was nothing between us but company for each other. My youngest daughter moved into my home, so I left all the furniture there for her. Our children visited us occasionally, but we did not receive many callers in a social sense. The servant I had hired stayed with us and took care of our needs. I had also hired a man to care for the farm.

I made a will, leaving Many Leaves well cared for. Everything else was left to Slow Bear's and my children to share equally. I left the property that Peter and Rain lived on to them. I left the property where the wagon building plant was situated to Mr. Coolidge. The rest of the property that was not owned by Seagram and the new mill owner I left to both Seagram and Coolidge.

I felt that I had now arranged for the disposal of everything I possessed after my death. That event occurred when I was seventy-eight years of age, due to a heart problem. I passed away peacefully in my sleep. Death had been my constant companion the past few years when most of my family passed away. I felt that he waited for me to be ready.

Death is not his proper name. Rather, he should be called the Transporter, because that is what he does. He transports the Soul from one plane of consciousness to another and does it with care and compassion, as the Great Spirit planned.

The End

Epilogue

This has been a difficult story to write. There was more heartache here than these words can adequately describe. When some situations were discussed, I did not want to include them in the book, but I was told by my Informants that I was acting as a judge and jury or a censor, and this was not my right. I was particularly concerned with some of the sexual matters described, then realized my work was to write what I was given and let others judge it for themselves.

Some names of people and places have been changed to protect the descendants that are still living. Indians do not give their names easily. They consider names to be private matter and will not give them out. Many Indians have several names and even a secret one that they never divulge.

When an Indian dies it is nearly impossible for those living to say that person's name. When they must, they merely whisper it. They do this in the belief that the Spirit of the dead person can do them harm, for it does not want its name spoken.

When an Indian dies, bowls of food are left nearby so the Spirit of that person will have food for his journey to the land of the Great Spirit. They believe that every living thing has a Spirit of its own. It is the Spirit of the food that is placed there that the Spirit of the dead person uses. They also believe that every object that the dead person made and used during his lifetime has been infused with a part of himself. This is why these things are buried with them. If objects can't be burned, they are broken and buried.

There are probably sections of this book that disagree with the accepted history of the Indians. This is because the stories that have been handed down to us were written by the White Man from his own perspective, not the Indian's. Perhaps this would change if the Indians could tell their own story, which I have tried to do. Some tales have been told about the noble Indian and his goodness and how badly he was treated. He *was* treated badly, but not all Indians were noble and some were not good. There are good and bad people in every race, and the Indians had their share of both.

Ignorance of people make us fear them. We now feel guilty about the way we have treated those we did not understand. I hope this book dispels some of this ignorance, so we can get on to where we respect one another and give all peoples the dignity they rightly deserve.

— George McMullen

About the Author

George McMullen was born in Woodbridge, Ontario, Canada, on January 14, 1920. Seeking to avoid ridicule, he kept his psychic gifts secret from the public until he was in his forties.

In 1969 he began working with J. Norman Emerson, Ph.D., an anthropologist/archaeologist at the University of Toronto. For more than 10 years, from 1969 until Dr. Emerson's death in 1978, the two men did research at various Indian sites in southern Ontario, Ohio, and New York state. Dr. Emerson described McMullen's work in numerous papers delivered to professional groups.

McMullen has traveled extensively in Canada and the United States, as well as to Egypt, Israel, France, England, Mexico, Honduras and Ecuador. He traveled in Egypt and Iran with a group headed by Hugh Lynn Cayce of the Edgar Cayce Foundation, researching Cayce's statements regarding those areas. He also worked in Egypt with the Mobius Group, a research organization based in Los Angeles, California. His work there is prominently featured in explorer/author Stephan Schwarz's two books *The Secret Vaults of Time* and *The Alexandria Project*.

McMullen has done extensive criminological work in several states with Ray Worring and Whitney Hibbard, which the two have mentioned in the books they have co-authored, *Psychic Criminology* and *Forensic Hypnosis*.

Articles about George McMullen have appeared in *Fate*, *MacLean Magazine*, *Canadian Heritage Magazine*, and many others.

He continues to work with archaeologists, criminologists and psychic explorers. He and his wife Charlotte currently live in British Columbia.

His first book, *Red Snake*, captivated readers with its details of the life of a 17th-century Huron. *One White Crow* seeks to shed light on how such a book as *Red Snake* can be authentic. And his third book, *Running Bear*, continues the series with the story of the grandson of Red Snake.

BOOKS OF RELATED INTEREST

RED SNAKE
George McMullen

In the first book of the series, McMullen, a psychic who became famous for his work in psychic archaeology, here relates the life of a Huron who lived in the days before the coming of the white Europeans—as told psychically by Red Snake himself. A simple, but compelling story of the thought processes of the American Indian in the eighteenth century.

"Fascinating in-depth look at the life of early Native American Woodlands people." — New Age Retailer

5¼ x 8¼ trade paper, 152 pages, ISBN 1-878901-58-3, $9.95

RUNNING BEAR
Grandson of Red Snake
George McMullen

Psychic archaeologist George McMullen carries the history of Red Snake's Huron family into the 1700s with the life story of Running Bear, who was fated to witness the destruction of the Native Americans' way of life. Orphaned, his village destroyed, Running Bear wanders through a land increasingly poisoned by White conflicts and passions. A truly remarkable description of a world in transition.

"Paints a vivid picture of the transition from a native culture living in harmony with nature to one out of sync with its rhythms." — Leading Edge Review

5 x 8 trade paper, 168 pages, ISBN 1-57174-037-6, $10.95

ONE WHITE CROW
George McMullen

Dr. Norman Emerson was one of Canada's pre-eminent archaeologists who, unlike many of his colleagues, readily reported the results of his forays into "intuitive archaeology." His collaborator, George McMullen, has here collected and republished Emerson's papers, with his own after-the-fact comments. A fascinating look at how psychic information and classic archaeology can work together to produce tangible results.

5½ x 8½ trade paper, 164 pages, ISBN 1-57174-007-4, $8.95

MY LIFE AFTER DYING
George G. Ritchie, Jr. M.D.
Introduction by Ian Stevenson, M.D.

"George Ritchie's story of his dying and coming back to life after some magnificent spiritual experiences is worth reading by all those who have any concern in the 'beyond.' To know that he was the inspiration that started Raymond Moody on his series of investigations into the afterlife makes him noteworthy."
— Spiritual Frontier

5½ x 8½ trade paper, 152 pages, ISBN 1-878901-25-7, $9.95

PAST LIVES, FUTURE GROWTH
Armand Marcotte and Ann Druffel

Psychic Armand Marcotte helps people with their problems, ranging from incest, suicide, and violent crimes to problems of marriage and divorce. Interestingly, he frequently finds that people's problems are rooted in previous lifetimes. *Past Lives, Future Growth* tells some of these stories.

5½ x 8½ trade paper, 202 pages, ISBN 1-878901-79-6, $8.95

MIND TREK
Joe McMoneagle

In the past year, Joe McMoneagle has been featured on ABC's *Nightline: Psychic Spies*, on the UPN Network program Paranormal Borderline, and in articles in *Time* and *Newsweek* that explored the DIA and CIA's use of remote viewers for psychic spying and locating kidnapped and missing service personnel. Remote viewing is the ability to "see" in the mind's eye things that are remote in time and/or space.

In the ABC special *Put to the Test*, McMoneagle amazed a national television audience by accurately remote viewing a randomly selected site under strict scientific protocol. Linton Weeks of the *Washington Post* says McMoneagle "put his skills on the line...and the demonstration was impressive."

Mind Trek gives guidelines on how to develop or enhance your own remote viewing skills.

"The reader learns the ins and outs of RV (remote viewing) with the help of a world-class practitioner."
— Brain/Mind

5½ x 8½ trade paper, 232 pages, ISBN 1-878901-72-9, $10.95

ANCIENT ECHOES
The Anasazi Book of Chants
Mary Summer Rain

The Anasazi people lived in the "four corners" area of the Southwest from A.D. 100 to 1300. Retrieved by spiritual memory, these chants express the heart of one sacred Anasazi community called the Spirit Clan. In addition to their great beauty, they also have practical uses; there are, for example, healing chants, marriage songs, a broken heart chant, a medicine prayer, and a child sleep song.

"Made me look at life and see how I could change it; to become closer to 'Grandfather and Mother Earth.'"
—Friend's Review

5½ x 8½ trade paper, 216 pages, ISBN 1-878901-87-7, $10.95

PHANTOMS AFOOT
Helping the Spirits Among Us
Mary Summer Rain

Mary Summer Rain's Indian teacher showed her how to use the power and follow the path of a dreamwalker. Under her guidance, Mary confronts wayward spirits who inhabit a timeless dimension between spiritual planes and helps them move on to other realities. In the process she learns of our spiritual obligation to all life.

5½ x 8½ trade paper, 336 pages, ISBN 1-878901-64-8, $12.95

THE DIVISION OF CONSCIOUSNESS
The Secret Afterlife of the Human Psyche
Peter Novak

After death, do we cross over to an afterlife? Or are we reborn to live another life here? Western and Eastern philosophies have disagreed on this point for thousands of years.

Novak argues that each perspective is partially correct. Drawing on mythology, psychology, religion, and science, as well as past-life regression and near-death experiences, he concludes that the human psyche divides at death, with the conscious mind reincarnating and the unconscious mind judging itself.

This stunningly simple premise explains the differences between many of the world's great religious sects. Further, Novak describes how this division may have arisen—and how it is likely to be resolved!

"The author's conclusions about the soul's survival of death are original, gripping, and so controversial that they will leave the reader feeling slightly stunned."
— Colin Wilson, author of The Philosopher's Stone

6 x 9 trade paper, 264 pages, ISBN 1-57174-053-8, $14.95

Hampton Roads Publishing Company
publishes and distributes books on a variety of subjects,
including metaphysics, health, complementary medicine,
visionary fiction, and other related topics.

To order or receive a copy of our latest catalog, call toll-free,
(800) 766-8009, or send your name and address to:

Hampton Roads Publishing Company, Inc.
134 Burgess Lane
Charlottesville, VA 22902